Kendall found an open spot along the boat's railing and turned to watch the sunset.

Before he realized what he was doing, Brice's feet ate up the distance between the steering wheel and Kendall and he joined her. Her gaze was fixed on the setting sun, her eyes wide and mouth slightly parted. She was beautiful, and for the first time since they began this venture together, he wished he was one of the guys on the date instead of running the event. If he'd brought Kendall, he'd have his arm around her right now.

He shook his thoughts away and moved to put space between them, but Kendall reached over and slipped her fingers over his wrist. "Stay."

He nodded and swallowed against the lump in his throat. What was he doing to himself? Kendall had made it clear that she didn't want a relationship with any man. She'd said she'd left dating in the past. He had, too.

She turned toward him and whispered, "We did good, didn't we?"

"Better than good." His words came out hoarse.

Jessica Keller is a Starbucks drinker, avid reader and chocolate aficionado. Jessica holds degrees in communications and biblical studies. She is multipublished in both romance and young-adult fiction and loves to interact with readers through social media. Jessica lives in the Chicagoland suburbs with her amazing husband, beautiful daughter and two annoyingly outgoing cats who happen to be named after superheroes. Find all her contact information at jessicakellerbooks.com.

Books by Jessica Keller

Love Inspired

Goose Harbor

The Widower's Second Chance
The Fireman's Secret
The Single Dad Next Door
Small-Town Girl

Home for Good

Small-Town Girl

Jessica Keller

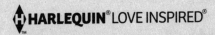

Recycling programs
for this product may
not exist in your area.

LOVE INSPIRED BOOKS

ISBN-13: 978-0-373-71973-0

Small-Town Girl

Copyright © 2016 by Jessica Koschnitzky

www.Harlequin.com

Printed in U.S.A.

Those who know Your name trust in You, for You, Lord, have never forsaken those who seek You.
—*Psalms* 9:10

For Kristen, who "gets it." Always.

Chapter One

Kendall Mayes shoved the freshly signed contract papers into her purse as she turned the corner and walked through the main section of downtown Goose Harbor.

She couldn't hold back her grin.

Love on a Dime—the business she had dreamed about for so many years—was going to open. *Next week*. According to the contract, all she had to do was stay silent about her business partner and find a weekly outing that would attract tourists. The weekly outing hadn't been part of her original business plan, but she could see why Sesser Atwood, her business partner, insisted it was needed. Success wouldn't come her way simply by waiting for people who wanted events and dates planned for them. A weekly event people could sign up for in advance translated into a more predictable income flow.

Her heels clipped against the bricked sidewalk. The businesses in downtown Goose Harbor were all situated around a large, grassy parklike square at the heart of the town and then fanned out down the streets that branched off the edges of the square.

Now one of those businesses was hers.

Building 836 boasted a slightly curved path made with round pavers that was lined on each side by an intricately carved wooden bench. Kendall traced her finger over the top of the nearest bench. They were beautiful. A mint-and-cherry awning hung above a door that opened to a tiny entryway leading to two more doors. The front door was heavy and squeaked a little when she opened it. The building was divided into two rentable spaces. Love on a Dime would take up residence on the left side, and a sign reading Goose Harbor Furniture let her know who her neighbor was on the other side.

The sweet smell of sawdust wafted from Goose Harbor Furniture's propped-open door. Reaching into her pocket, Kendall closed her hand around the key Sesser had handed her after their meeting. Trepidation gnawed away at the pit of her stomach. This was it.

Laying her other hand on the door, Kendall bowed her head. She didn't pray as often as she should, but then again, she found it difficult to think of the right words when it felt as if they never made it past the ceiling. Kendall was one girl among millions. The daily issues she faced didn't matter to the creator of the universe, did they? No. If her earthly father had been able to walk out of her life and forget about her, God could too.

Still, she had to believe that God had led local tycoon Sesser Atwood to overhear the bank turning down her application for a business loan. If the elderly man hadn't asked to hear her pitch and then offered to go into business with her, Kendall would be on her way back to Kentucky by now.

Thank You for bringing me here. For orchestrating all this. If it's not too much to ask, please let this be a place I can call home. Finally.

She slipped the key into the old-fashioned doorknob and opened the door. The tiniest bell, hung on the upper part of the door, rang sweetly as she entered. A note taped to the desk from Claire, Sesser's adult daughter, read that she had picked out the furniture and decorations and hoped Kendall liked everything. The furniture was meant as a gift, partner-to-partner. The note ended with a huge smiley face. Kendall started adding up the costs in her head and was beginning to wonder if she'd ever be able to pay Sesser back if she had to. Could Mr. Atwood really be so generous? Hopefully it came without strings, but in her experience, gifts rarely did. Especially gifts from wealthy men.

On a separate note card Claire had written a verse in her pretty, swirling script. Kendall ran her thumb over the card, reading Isaiah 43:19 out loud. "'See, I am doing a new thing. Now it springs up; do you not perceive it? I am making a way in the wilderness and streams in the desert.'" Finding a thumbtack, she stuck the verse onto the corkboard near her monitor. Claire didn't know her, but she couldn't have picked a better verse to encourage Kendall. Perhaps God did care about something as insignificant as Kendall's dreams.

She laid her purse on the desk and was just about to turn on the computer when an awful screeching sound vibrated the walls. "Oh. That's not going to work at all."

Instantly she started for the door leading to the shared entryway. A high-pitched beeping sound echoed as she walked through the furniture store's front door.

Goose Harbor Furniture consisted of two sections; one area showcased completed handmade pieces and items that were ready to purchase, and the other was full of sawdust and half-finished projects. In the middle, two men hunched over a block of wood. One was wielding a power saw, which explained the noise.

"Excuse me!" Kendall hollered.

Both men turned in her direction. The taller, broader-shouldered man had sandy-brown, close-cropped hair, a firm jaw and a tug of a smile on his lips. His heavy boots, worn jeans and rolled-up flannel shirt screamed *hard work*. The shorter of the two had floppy brown hair and a full-blown grin lighting his boyish features. But what struck her most was both men had the same unique eye coloring. A pale green, like the underside of a leaf.

Thankfully the smaller-statured one switched off the saw before swiveling around. "If you're here for the whittling class, tonight's lesson is canceled on account of the concert in the square."

She quirked an eyebrow. "Whittling? No." She shook her head. "I'm here about that horrible noise."

The taller one walked forward. "Brice Daniels." He extended his hand for a handshake, the calluses along his palm rubbing against her soft skin. "Back there—" Brice jutted a thumb over his shoulder toward the man with the saw "—is my brother Evan. He owns this place. You can blame him for all the racket."

"I'm Kendall. Kendall Mayes." She laid her hand across her chest. "Nice to meet you both." Then she zeroed in on Evan. "Do you normally use that during business hours?"

He set down the saw and then hooked his hands on his tool belt. "Hey, it's almost closing time."

Kendall popped her hands to her hips. "Well, I'm your new neighbor, and I don't know how that's going to affect my clients." Her small office would mostly be used for planning, but she had to imagine that potential clients would want to be able to meet with her in a saw-free environment. Had Sesser been aware of the woodworker next door when he chose this location for her? If Evan was going to be carving loudly all day, she might not last in the shared storefront for long.

"Relax." Evan unclipped his tool belt and laid it on the workstation in the back of the room. "The tools I mostly use are quiet. The saw is used sparingly and only ever before the shop opens or near closing."

Kendall released a breath she hadn't realized she was holding.

Brice tilted his head, considering her. "I spotted you at church last weekend, didn't I? You're new in town." He had a slight cleft in his chin. Kendall tried not to stare, but there was no doubt about it; the man was an all-American hunk.

"I am." She offered a smile. "Is it so easy to tell?"

Evan peeled off his heavy gloves. "We're Goose Harbor lifers. Born and raised. We know almost everyone."

"You grew up here?" Kendall's attention volleyed between the brothers. What must it have been like to live in such a picturesque place? Probably far better than the trailer homes she and her mother had constantly been kicked out of for not paying rent. "That must have been nice."

"At times. But not always." Brice leaned against

the counter that held the cash register and crossed his arms.

Kendall took a few steps, pretending to examine the furniture for sale. "So, what's this about a whittling class?"

Straightening, Brice grabbed the stapler off the counter and twisted it around in his hand. His gaze quickly appraised her from head to toe. "You don't strike me as someone interested in whittling."

"Don't listen to him." Evan rounded the small partition that separated the woodworking area from the store. "He doesn't even work here."

"Okay." Kendall put up her hands in surrender. "The truth is, I'm not interested in whittling at all. But I just had an idea. I'm trying to brainstorm some events that I could offer for tourists…on a weekly basis in correlation with my business." Not that whittling would be the most exciting thing, but she didn't know anyone besides a handful of ladies from a Bible study she'd attended for a few weeks when she first moved to town and she was currently grasping at straws. Sesser expected her to kick off her business with a bang and she didn't want to disappoint him. Not after the risk he'd taken on her.

"It's a paid class that meets once a week and runs six weeks long. Most of the tourists are only here for a week or two, tops. There's the occasional ones that stay for the whole season. But they're few and far between." Evan shrugged an apology.

Kendall sighed. Whittling wouldn't work for her weekly event. Which was probably for the best.

Brice cleared his throat. "Maybe I can help point

you in the right direction? What sort of business are you starting next door?"

Here it goes. She took a deep breath and squared her shoulders. While Kendall really believed in her idea, embarrassment always rolled around in her chest whenever she had to explain it. Most people didn't understand the need for such a place. "It's called Love on a Dime. It's a date-planning service, and—"

"Hear that? A dating service." Evan slapped Brice on the back. "She can finally find you a match."

Brice shot his brother a look that said *if the lady wasn't here right now I'd strangle you.* "I don't date."

She waved her hands. "I don't find significant others for people. None of that matching stuff. I plan dates for people who are already together." Despite Brice's scowl, she rambled on. "So, say a man wants to take his girlfriend out on a fun date but doesn't want to fuss with the details. I step in and take care of everything."

Eyebrows diving, Brice worked his jaw back and forth. "So some guy can spend a bunch of money to impress a girl who will just dump him later on?"

Well, that went horribly.

"Some people actually end up happy and married." Not her. Or anyone she knew very well. But that didn't stop her from hoping it was true. Kendall blew out a long stream of air that ruffled her dark bangs. "Anyway. I wanted to introduce myself and make sure that sound wasn't going to be a constant thing. Since you said it's not, I'll head back to my place and try to accomplish something before locking up for the night. Nice meeting you both."

She retreated to her side before either of them could get in another word. Rounding her desk, she dropped into the rolling chair and pressed her face into her hands.

Five weeks ago she'd sold more than half of her possessions and moved to a town she'd never visited before to open a new business. Her home back in Kentucky hadn't been the type of place to attract tourists, and the pull for a business like hers there was almost nonexistent. There was one small country club in her hometown where she'd worked, but that would have been the extent of her clientele. In Goose Harbor, where new tourists flooded the streets each week of the summer, the possibility for work was endless.

But had it all been another mistake waiting to happen? Would everyone react the way Brice had? One more thing to add to the list of failures she'd experienced in her life?

Kendall prayed for guidance but only heard the murmur of the Daniels brothers talking next door.

Brice grabbed the broom out of the back room and started sweeping the sawdust from his brother's latest creation into a pile. He'd already put in a full day's work down at his shipping business near the dock but hadn't felt like going back to his empty cabin after he sent his men home for the day. The cryptic voice mail from his father on his business's answering machine might have something to do with that.

Evan locked the front door and grinned at Brice. "She's cute."

"Leave the poor woman alone, Evan." Brice shook his head. His brother always showered attention on attractive women. Actually the trait had gotten Evan into trouble far too many times in his life. The whispers even reached the docks. Women visiting Goose Harbor loved batting their eyes at Brice's younger brother. There were some who came a few months each summer trying to win Evan over. Little did they know, Evan was a lost cause where love was concerned. Brice had been around and seen the women in action, though. His brother didn't shy from their attention, and—right or wrong—it brought him sales.

"Admit it." Evan nudged him in the ribs. "You thought she was cute too."

Evan had always been considered the best-looking and most charismatic of the Daniels brothers. Not that he had much competition when compared to only Brice. Most people had forgotten or chose not to talk about their middle brother, Andrew, who took off years ago. Brice hadn't heard from him in a good four years. He clenched his fist. Their little sister, Laura, hadn't even been ten years old when Andrew left. How could his brother have done that to the family?

Brice found the dustpan and filled it twice. "You know better than me—cute is dangerous."

His brother watched him work for a moment before speaking. "Not every woman is Audra."

Brice winced. While thoughts of Audra didn't bother him any longer, he still wanted to avoid that part of his life. Love had the same effect on the heart as a stingray barb did. It hurt and had the potential of killing something inside a man that didn't ever want to be revived again.

"I didn't come here to talk to you about women."

Evan cocked his head and clearly fought a smile. "Half the time you act like you're allergic to all of humanity and hole yourself up in your cabin all alone.

Tonight you just *happen* to wander down to my shop in the heart of where the tourists hang out. I know you too well. You wouldn't be here unless you had something serious to talk about."

Brice scrubbed his hand over his aching jaw. His TMJ was acting up again. "How many times do I have to tell you that introverts don't necessarily dislike people, we just prefer being alone more?"

"There are introverts and then there are hermits." Evan held up both hands like a scale. "You, brother, lean much closer to the second category, I'm afraid. But that's neither here nor there. What do you need?"

Brice's brother had always possessed an ability to read people. Or maybe it only worked where Brice was concerned, since he and Evan had been through so much together. Brothers couldn't spend hours as children huddled under piles of clothes in their closet, praying their father's rampage ended before he found them, without becoming close.

Tell Evan about Dad's voice mail? No. Not today.

Brice shoved his hands deep into his pockets. "I need advice."

"All right." Evan hopped up so he was seated on top of the counter by the register. "Shoot."

"My business is in trouble."

Evan's eyes grew wide. "What kind of trouble? Do you need money? I could—"

Brice stopped Evan's words by holding up his hands. "I didn't come here to ask you for money. I hate admitting it, but I think I bit off more than I can chew. I'm not in serious trouble—at least not yet—but I could be soon if business keeps going in the direction it's heading right now."

"Are you behind on bills?"

"Not yet."

"Listen." Evan slid back down so he was standing on the floor. He crossed the room so he was inches away from Brice and lowered his voice. "Don't mess with Sesser. Whatever you do, promise me you won't go into debt to that man. He will... Just don't get in debt to him."

"Evan, I know what he did to you. I won't—"

"Promise me." Evan growled the words through clenched teeth. A vein on his neck bulged.

Brice dropped a hand onto his brother's shoulder. "I won't go into debt to the likes of him. You know I wouldn't do that. I'd lose my house and move in with your hide before missing a payment to that man."

"Good." Evan lifted his shoulders, making Brice's hand fall, and strode away from him. "So, what— *exactly*—is going on?"

"When I first started, shipments were good. But last winter was colder than normal and there was less of a demand. Last summer, since things seemed to be going well, I purchased more boats. And not just barges, all different kinds. If business had kept up like it had been, I would have been able to start socking away money. But it didn't. Do you know how expensive upkeep on a boat is?"

Evan shrugged and glanced around his furniture shop. "Costs a lot more than buying wood."

"And if those boats are just sitting in dock, taking a space that I have to pay for and not doing anything... they become a red line in my accounting books."

"You still use actual books? The sort with paper and pens?"

"Stay on topic, will you?"

"Sorry. Too many boats."

"Better." Brice turned away from his brother and watched the people seated outside, on vacation, joking with one another. Had he ever taken a break or just gone away from home? Not other than college… and that could hardly have been considered a break. "I think I need to start selling off my boats and cut my fleet to just the two or three that are constantly in use. Then I'll just pray that none of them break down."

Short term, the unused boats might be a problem, but they only masked what truly bothered him. Sesser Atwood was the real issue.

What Brice wouldn't give to get out from under that millionaire's thumb. Everything the man touched turned bad. Made money, sure. But Atwood's influence corrupted and did so absolutely. The man cared about success and compounding his money and nothing more. Paying rent to the man for space at the dock irked Brice more than he cared to admit, but other than moving, there'd been no other option when he first started his shipping company.

And moving from Goose Harbor was out of the question. At least while his younger sister still lived at home with his unstable parents. Brice needed to stay nearby, be there for her and take the brunt of their parents' emotional outbursts whenever he could. He'd done the same for his brothers as much as he could. Besides, Brice knew a thing or two about bullies. He would put up with Sesser's antics for as long as Laura needed him to.

Which left Brice with no other options. Sesser owned the moorings in Shadowbend, the next town over, as well as Goose Harbor. The property on the other side of town was a state preserve, so no docks there. He would have to go twenty miles up or down the lake in order to dock somewhere the tycoon didn't own, and that put him too far from his little sister if there was an emergency.

The problem was Sesser charged as many fees as he could think up. It didn't matter if a ship was taking something away or dropping off goods—Sesser collected money for both. He was the kind of man who walked the line between legal and illegal business dealings but had enough powerful friends in the state that it didn't matter if he sometimes tipped too far into the illegal.

A sharp pain along the side of his face made Brice realize he was clenching his back molars together. He forced himself to relax with a deep breath. Hadn't his doctor threatened him with surgery if he didn't stop grinding his teeth and clenching his jaw all the time?

Too many years spent swallowing words could do that to a man.

Someday Brice would break free of Sesser Atwood and then he'd never deal with the man again. He'd watched Atwood destroy his father, scare his mother and steamroll his youngest brother's one chance at happiness.

Brice wasn't about to let the old businessman ruin him too.

"Selling the boats could work." Evan braced his hands on the counter. "Or you could expand your business."

"That's what got me into trouble in the first place."

"Not like you're thinking. I mean find more work."

"Believe me, I've tried to secure every contract on Lake Michigan. I've done everything to—"

"Sure, every *shipping* contract, but that's not what I'm talking about. Think of something else to use the boats for."

"Like?"

"Hey, just a simple woodworker here." Evan held up his hands in mock surrender. "I can encourage you. Not actually come up with the ideas on the fly."

Brice had considered using his boats for fishing tours. But fishing tours were hours of commitment. And this wasn't the Caribbean. The fish in Lake Michigan might be huge, but there wasn't all that impressive an assortment to be found.

"Fishing tours?" He tossed the words out to see what his brother would say.

Evan tapped his chin, thinking for a second. "That has merit. Although you'd have to hire someone to give the tours, and that would cost money."

"I could do them. I know where the best fish—"

"You are many things, but a friendly tour guide is not one of them."

"Maybe I'll just sell the boats. Admit my losses and downsize." He had a smattering of small vessels he'd picked up secondhand. They weren't hauling boats, but he'd figured they'd be useful for something. So far, they'd been nothing but money pits. He'd sell them. Let them become someone else's problems.

Evan opened his cash register and removed the drawer of money. "That could work too, and there's no shame in that plan, but will it ruin you to give yourself one week to brainstorm a few other possible solutions?"

"A week's not going to ruin me."

"Then go back to that cabin of yours and think."

At this time on a summer evening, the main part of downtown Goose Harbor was flooded with people, so much so that cars stopped driving down the roads because there were too many pedestrians to maneuver around. Besides, Brice had left his car by the docks. He'd exit out the back door of Evan's business and cut across the beach. He needed to spend some time seeking out God's guidance anyway. The less-congested evening beach would be the perfect place to go pray.

The short-lease condo that Kendall had found to rent when she first moved to town was located on the opposite end of Ring Beach from the main portion of town. Walking to her business meeting with Sesser and Claire had sounded like a great idea earlier, but now her feet ached. Heels weren't built for cross-terrain travel.

A girl from the foothills of Kentucky would need to ease into beach living slowly. Even if it was only a freshwater beach on Lake Michigan, having never been to the ocean, she found it the biggest, most impressive beach she'd ever seen.

Which was one of the reasons why she'd chosen Goose Harbor as the perfect place to start her business. Sure, a place like Orlando or Los Angeles would have been ideal, but then again, they would have been far too pricey. Her savings wouldn't have lasted long in one of those cities. Rent the first month or two would have drained her completely. Moreover, her little business would have been easy to overlook in a large city.

She could have never marketed enough to get noticed somewhere big.

After seeing the article in *Midwestern Travel* magazine about the quaint tourist town of Goose Harbor that swelled to four times its population for six months of the year, she knew she'd found her location. Her dream could finally become a reality. Discovering that Ring Beach was one of two freshwater beaches in the whole country that made it onto a list of best beaches in the world—well, that information sealed the deal.

A place like Goose Harbor would draw lots of couples and people looking for romance. That was where Love on a Dime would step in and plan dates for them. Provide whole catalogs of choices for clueless men looking to impress their girlfriends or, better yet, plan their proposals. And when no one was in the market for a date, she'd offer event-planning services or book excursions for girls' weekends. The process had become second nature after she'd worked as an event planner at the golf course near her hometown for the past eight years.

She often wondered how many of the weddings she'd overseen ended in divorce. Fifty percent—that was the going rate nowadays, right? The number never ceased to shock her as well as solidify her desire not to marry. She'd been right to leave her serial dating habits back in Kentucky. Men complicated things. No, actually sometimes men were quite useful. Like when heavy boxes were involved.

Love was the enemy more than anything. Love made a person foolish and far too trusting. Love was responsible for countless people getting taken advantage of. But not her. Thankfully she had always ended her relationships before they became too serious. Goose Harbor would be a baggage-free paradise for her.

"Wait up." A voice behind her made her stop.

She turned around to find Brice Daniels a few feet away.

"Oh, hey. It's Brice, right?"

"Yes." A quick wince crossed his face before he masked it. Brice looked tired, or like he had something on his mind.

"Are you okay?"

"Just wondering why you're so determined to cross this beach with those shoes on when the sand's cooled down some by now." He smiled, but the look didn't reach those piercing, pale green eyes of his.

"But the sun's only just setting." She turned toward the lake, pointing at the sun, but then stopped and grabbed Brice's solid arm. There was no adequate way to describe the beauty of the sun going down over the lake, so instead Kendall gasped. "Sit and watch this with me." She tugged on his sleeve.

Brice didn't argue. He dropped onto the sand and looped his arms over his knees. "It never gets old, does it?"

Kendall sat right beside him and watched the orange and magenta light dance with the coming night across the lake's surface. "I've never seen a sunset quite like this. It's…it's…too much for words."

"You should see it out on the lake."

"I can." She thrust her hand out to indicate the water.

"From a boat."

"When I find someone with a boat, I will."

"I own a whole fleet of them."

Shifting her gaze from the sunset to Brice, she caught him staring at her. "Would you take me some-time?"

"Sure." He shrugged.

"Soon."

"Okay."

"Tomorrow?"

Brice chuckled. "All right."

Wait. Had she just forced him to take her on a date? Wow. Her forward personality always seemed to get her into trouble. But she hoped it didn't come across that way. No. She hadn't…right? She couldn't, because Kendall was not dating anymore. Goose Harbor was going to be a boyfriend-free zone.

Kendall trailed her fingers through the sand. "If you don't want to, that's fine. I kind of forced that on you."

He looked over at her and they made eye contact. "I want to." His voice was soft, almost a whisper. Brice's pale green eyes were so intense her breath caught for a heartbeat. He kept speaking. "I have some smaller boats that I need to test out. I'm trying to decide what to do with them. One is nicer, and I've only taken it out once since I bought it. She could use a spin out on the lake."

"She?"

"All boats are women. I thought that was common knowledge."

"I guess I don't spend time with enough pirates to know these things about boats."

"You slay me." He laid his hand on his heart. "Do you see an eye patch or a peg leg here?"

"You're right. Pirates certainly don't use words like *slay*."

"Blame the books for how I talk."

"You're a reader?" She wondered what types of books he read. Nonfiction books about fixing cars? Autobiographies about people who definitely weren't pirates? Or did strong Brice Daniels curl up with a fictional mystery during his downtime? Her interest piqued, suddenly she wanted to know all about him.

"Of course." Brice's voice broke through her thoughts. "What else is there to do when you're out on the lake?"

"Um, watch these amazing sunsets!" She slapped his arm but then left her hand there. "Brice, I was just hit with the most amazing idea. Care to hear me out?"

"Sure." Another one-word answer.

"You don't speak a ton, do you?"

"That's what you wanted to talk about?"

"No, but I just thought that."

"Do you say everything you think right when you think it?"

Kendall pursed her lips and rubbed her chin, pretending to think really hard for effect. It worked. Brice shook his head, a half grin on his face and his eyes twinkling with a shared joke.

"Okay." Kendall rolled her eyes. "Most of the time I say exactly what I'm thinking. Right when I think it."

"Well, I don't."

"That's it?"

"Yeah, I guess." Even with his boots on, he moved his feet back and forth in the sand as if he was digging in his toes. "I believe in thinking about things and not always saying them out loud. Words don't always solve problems."

"But sometimes they do."

"Sometimes silence is better."

"I feel sorry for your girlfriend." Kendall slapped her hand over her mouth. "Wow. Sorry. That didn't come out like it sounded in my head."

Brice raised his eyebrows, but the lift at the edge of his lips told her he wasn't mad.

Kendall pinched the bridge of her nose. "All right, you win. Sometimes silence is better, like it would have been four seconds ago. Let's silently sit here and watch the sunset. Then we can silently walk across the beach. Afterward, we can silently say goodbye to each other. Won't that be fun?"

"Why don't you tell me your idea first? The one you had before getting off track."

"I will. But sorry about the girlfriend thing. I'm sure she's happy and—"

"I don't have one, so no worries. No wives in the attic either."

"*Jane Eyre* reference. Nicely done." She sent him a wink.

Brice inched toward her. "Your idea?"

Kendall scooted so she was facing him. "Sunset cruises."

"Yes…we're doing one tomorrow."

"Not just tomorrow. What if we had a planned sunset cruise every single week?"

His eyes grew wide. "You and me?"

"Well, yes, we'd both be there, but I'm talking about hosting it as a tourist activity. Every Friday night— Scratch that." Kendall gathered up her hair and bunched it at the nape of her neck to keep the wind from whipping it around. "I'm sure there are better things you want to do on your Friday nights than spend them with me. Any night of the week would work really, as long as it was the same night each week so people could count on it. We'd charge a set fee and host a sunset cruise out onto the lake."

Brice rocked a bit and leaned onto his elbows. He worked his jaw back and forth for a minute.

She'd gone too far, hadn't she? Presumed upon this poor man who was now trying to find the kindest words he could to let her down. She always did this, didn't she? Plowing ahead before thinking things through had only ever gotten her in trouble. And it made her a risk that most men didn't want to be around. Like dynamite. They never knew when the risk would be too great or her ideas lead to failures.

This trait was probably what had driven her father to walk out on her and her mother when she was only six. Too much energy. Too many ideas. Too many failures.

Brice still hadn't spoken up. She needed to take him out of his misery. "I shouldn't have spouted that out like that. You don't know me, and I know nothing of your boating company. And the cruises probably wouldn't work, so—"

He finally sat up. "I think they will."

"You… Really?"

"There are some smaller, fancier boats in my fleet. I bought them on a whim at an auction without knowing what I'd do with them. They could work really well for something like this."

"You don't think my idea is silly?"

He shook his head. "Not at all. It might be the answer to the prayer I hadn't prayed yet."

"Is that even possible?"

Brice nodded solemnly. "God knows what we need."

Kendall flattened her hands against the cooled sand. "When should we start?"

"Let's rein this in for a minute. How about we go on our cruise tomorrow and get a better idea of everything before making plans? Deal?" He rose to his feet, dusted off his pants and then held out a hand to her, helping her stand.

"Deal."

They walked silently down the beach until they reached the edge, where they parted ways.

"I'll see you tomorrow." He headed toward the shipping yard.

"Until then." She waved over her shoulder and headed home for the evening with a lighter step. Perhaps Brice Daniels was right. Maybe God answered prayers people hadn't prayed yet.

Even hers.

Chapter Two

Kendall had changed her outfit. Six times.

It's not a date.

In the end, she opted for comfort over style and wore leopard-print ballet flats paired with skinny jeans and a charcoal tank top that had some fancy draping across the front.

This morning after unpacking her condo a little more, Kendall had headed to Love on a Dime, where she'd spent the day drafting a press release and brainstorming other ways to get the word out about her business now that it was officially open.

Next she'd looked up Brice online, since she'd forgotten to get his number last night, and found surprisingly little information. Unless he used a false name online—and he really didn't seem the type—he had no social-media accounts. His shipping business was called, get this: Brice Daniels. Just his name. At least that had made the number to his company easy to find. Her next move would have been bugging his brother next door, but Evan had been busy all afternoon entertaining a string of customers. She'd called Brice's number and left a message on what sounded like an ancient answering machine. His voice came across deeper on the greeting than she remembered.

He'd called her back at the office ten minutes later and they'd settled on a time to meet at the pier. And now it was time. Kendall bounced her shoulders up and down a few times to relax them. *Nerves.* From looking forward to another sunset and the possibility of having a way to meet Sesser's demand for a weekly event so easily; that was all.

Instead of walking the beach as she'd done yesterday, Kendall drove to the dock. Nothing was clearly marked and she couldn't find a parking spot, so she parked along the side of one of the warehouses where her vehicle wouldn't be in the way and headed out to find Brice. Kendall didn't have to walk too far onto the docks, though, because she spotted him waiting for her near the front of the pier. He waved and Kendall felt her breath catch.

Oh. Grow up already.

But it was impossible not to notice Brice's strong presence. His shoulders were wide and his profile cut an ideal male figure against the backdrop of boats lightly bobbing in the marina. He wore nicer boots than he'd had on yesterday. These ones were the kind that could be worn to church or to a casual office. Dark jeans, a formfitting gray Henley that looked as though it would be incredibly soft from many trips through the washing machine and a navy blue lightweight jacket completed his look. Kendall had to command her jaw to keep from dropping wide-open. She'd dated plenty of men in the past ten years, but none who looked as effortlessly handsome as Brice. The man belonged in a movie playing a dashing prince.

The sun hadn't set yet, but it would in the next half hour. For the most part, the pier was quiet. Gentle waves lapped back and forth against the moorings, and a few fat seagulls scavenged for food along the beach.

"Ready?" Brice's whole face lit up as he smiled.

"Lead the way."

He surprised her by offering his arm. She took it and they started down the pier. There were two places to dock boats in Goose Harbor—the white-painted wooden pier located near the downtown area that held all the fancy sailboats and yachts or the working pier, where they currently were. This one was concrete. It had stains and puddles and carried the smell of freshly caught fish. Most of the boats attached to the working pier were barges and other large ships. Here they were tucked away from the normal path and sight line of tourists. Toward the far right, one boat stuck out because it didn't look like the rest of them. It was white and green and had a deck sitting on top.

"Is that her?"

Brice nodded. "I know she needs to be spruced up before we can put the public on her, but I think this one will be the best in my fleet for the cruises. At least at the start."

"I think the biggest improvement will be moving it to the other pier in town. That should be first on our list."

Brice stopped walking. "Move it to the other pier?"

"Of course. That's the pier tourists know about and gather at. This pier is functional and all, but it's not pretty and won't do for running tours. You see that, don't you?" She felt the muscles in his arm flex under her hand as she spoke. Had she said something wrong?

He looked down the pier and took a deep breath. "You may have a point."

"Did I say something wrong?"

"It's fine. I try to deal as little as possible with the man who owns the piers, is all." Brice worked his free hand over his jaw. "But I'll see if there's space to rent at that one. I'll check into it tomorrow."

"Thank you."

He unwound her arm from his, pulled the edge of the boat so it came flush with the pier and opened the gate-like door. "In you go." He offered his hand again so he could help her across the gap of water, as the boat had already started drifting away from the pier a bit.

Kendall didn't wait for Brice to give her a tour. Instead she started through the boat on her own. It had two separate levels. The top had a green awning, and the bottom was contained but still above water. The lower section boasted wide windows so both levels could be used for a cruise if there were enough passengers. The lower level also had a small kitchen and two bathrooms.

After climbing the stairs to the upper level, Kendall spotted what appeared to be a huge wheel of red paddles at the back of the boat. It reminded her of something out of an old-time movie. She turned around to find that Brice had been trailing her.

"It's called a paddle wheeler. But it's a very small one."

"So it's like Tom Sawyer on the Mississippi River. You've just upped the cuteness level of this sunset cruise venture a hundredfold. People will love to snap pictures on this thing. People will go selfie crazy on this boat!" Joy bubbled up in her chest. As long as Brice agreed, this sunset cruise plan could work.

Brice tapped the boat. "I'm no expert on cuteness levels, so I'll take your word on that."

"Do you use this boat to haul things for your business?"

"I could. It has a lot of surface area for its size, so when it came up at the auction I placed a bid. Most people were there that day for heavy-duty working ships, so I got her for a good price. But it hasn't been used much since I bought her."

"Which turns out to be a good thing for us."

"A blessing in disguise." He smiled. "Ready to head out? The sun will be setting in the next twenty minutes here, and the lake is smooth enough to go out a ways."

Kendall grabbed the side railing and tried to jiggle it. "Are you sure she's sound?" That was a correct ship statement, right?

"She's sound. Needs a new coat of paint and an elbow grease of a cleaning, but she's sound. The coast guard certified her, and we'll have to have her inspected annually just like the rest of the ships. We'll have to carry more life jackets on board. I think she's got ten or so now, but we'll need one for every passenger we plan to have. The ship-to-shore radio worked the last time I checked, and she's radar-equipped."

"Then let's shove off." Kendall saluted him because that felt like the right thing to do to a boatman, but heat flashed across her cheeks after doing so.

Brice's face did that thing where he was clearly fighting a huge, goofy grin again. "Aye-aye, Captain."

He unwound the ropes holding the boat to the pier

and then jumped back onto the vessel. Brice worked
his way to the top of the ship, where there was a booth
built for him to sit at and steer. Kendall came alongside him as he started the boat and it rumbled to life.

Brice winked at her. "Go on over to the edge and
enjoy the ride."

Kendall made her way to the back near the paddles
and watched the red slats slap against the water as they
headed away from the sight of the little, safe harbor in
town and out into the waters of Lake Michigan. She
leaned against the railing and watched the town grow
smaller in the distance, wondering if she should have
asked Brice just how far out they were going to go.

After a while he angled the boat so it was going up
the shoreline, away from Goose Harbor and toward an
area full of dunes and a thick forest. When the leaves
changed yellow and brown in the fall, the hill probably
looked like a group of giant, sleeping bears.

"See them?" Brice hollered. He pointed down the
shore to a place near where a large river entered the
lake.

Kendall shaded her eyes with her hand. "See what?
The river?"

"The eagles!" Brice pointed again. "They're getting ready to fish."

She looked higher and then gasped. Three bald eagles soared in a circle high above the trees that grew
near the mouth of the river. Their wing spans were
huge. "I didn't know you had those in Michigan."

"We do." The boat started going much slower. "On
nights when the lake is too rough, we can offer a cruise
up that river instead. It's a protected area, but I called
the rangers today and they said river cruises are al-

lowed and welcome on the preserve. There's bound to be all sorts of wildlife to spot. I think most tourists would like that."

He'd called the rangers today? If Brice was thinking ahead, then he really was on board with running these sunset cruises and wasn't just being kind. He was an equal partner.

Wouldn't it be nice to finally be around someone she could count on? That wasn't a trait she usually associated with men in her life. Maybe Brice was different.

Or maybe she didn't know him well enough yet.

Brice turned off the paddle wheeler and dropped both the bow and stern anchors, which was probably overkill, but better safe than sorry.

He crossed the boat to where Kendall stood, watching him. Not knowing what to do, and more than anything not wanting to sound foolish in front of her, he chose to stand beside her and look out at the sunset. Kendall didn't make a move to talk right away. She simply turned and stood shoulder to shoulder with him. Her hand rested beside his on the rail, making his heart thump off-kilter in a way it hadn't done since college. Since the first time he saw Audra.

Brice stole a glance at Kendall. *Gorgeous.* Better than any sunset. He kept finding his gaze shifting back to her. Kendall's skin had an exotic color to it; he thought he'd heard that type of skin called olive toned before. Her hair was thick, and dark, and had soft-looking curls. Her nose had character. It was a little big, but it fit her perfectly. Maybe six inches shorter than him, she was a good height. If he tucked his arm around her, she'd fit perfectly into the crook of his body.

Brice pinched the bridge of his nose and squeezed his eyes shut.

What was he thinking?

Hadn't he been kicked in the teeth enough by women? He was not going to jump back into the dating pond anytime soon. Besides, women didn't care about being committed. They cared about what a guy had to offer them. They liked to be chased, not caught. He would do well to remember that he had nothing to offer to anyone; in fact, he usually made people's lives worse.

If I hadn't had you I wouldn't be stuck.

He took a step away from Kendall and from his mother's voice in his mind at the same time. When he opened his eyes, Kendall had followed his movement, though. She was looking up at him, wearing an open expression.

"You have a scar." She tapped his cheek where there had been a deep, half-inch scar since he was eight years old. From a belt buckle to the face. "I didn't notice it before."

He grabbed her hand and steered her back to the railing. "Don't miss the sunset."

Space. He just needed space.

Brice turned to head back to the inside of the boat, but Kendall snagged his arm.

"Stay with me. It's no fun watching this or dreaming about romance alone."

"Romance?" He reeled back a bit.

"Don't look so shocked. I'm not talking about us. Love on a Dime. My business. Remember?" She spent the next ten minutes as the sun sank lower detailing her plan-a-date service. Brice's resolve against dating grew stronger with each word she spoke. An entire business dedicated to making men spend money to impress their girlfriends? And his shipping business was going to be tangled up in it.

Yup, women worked exactly like he'd figured. Exactly as Audra—his last girlfriend—had. She'd done him a favor when she turned down his proposal. They would never have been happy together. Brice saw that now. But it didn't remove the sting of rejection, even all these years later.

Kendall's voice broke through his thoughts. "We should offer this as one of the date packages on top of running the weekly cruises. What do you think?"

"Not sure." He shoved his hands into his pockets. "I'll have to think on it a couple days if that's all right with you."

"Of course. It's your boat, so the choice is all yours. I just think that people would really pay well for this experience. And I'm meeting with a chef next week who I'm sure I could convince to cater meals for dates. Wouldn't it be romantic to eat here at the back of the boat while the sun set? The couples could finish the evening by dancing here under the stars." She closed her eyes for a second and swayed. "Does the boat have a sound system?"

"It does." His jaw was aching again. "How'd you come up with the idea to start your business?"

She bit her lip. "Want me to be completely honest?"

He scrubbed his hand over his face. "What else would I want?"

"Right. Silly question." Kendall broke eye contact. "Before I moved to Goose Harbor, I dated. A lot."

"Define 'a lot.'"

"A lot." She crossed her arms and looked back at him. "Nothing serious. But suffice to say, I've been on more dates than I can count." She uncrossed her arms and trailed her fingers absently on the railing. "Some of them were really creative, and I planned a lot of them, as well. In the midst of it I realized that I'm really great at the dating part of relationships, so why not make money off that? I used to work as an event planner for a small golf course near my hometown, and the idea sort of sprang from that."

She rubbed her hands back and forth over her bare arms. Although it was summer, the evenings cooled down quickly, especially out on the water. And she was only wearing a tank top of sorts.

Brice shrugged out of his coat. "Put this on. You've got to be cold."

"Thank you."

She slipped it on without hesitation, then pulled the collar up to her nose and breathed in. Did it smell bad? No—at least, her closing her eyes and breathing deeply again didn't suggest that.

"What kind of cologne do you wear?"

"I don't."

She gave him a look that said she thought he was lying. Brice held up his hands. "Bar soap. I promise that's the extent of it."

"Well, that's some great bar soap. I'm telling you." She pulled the coat tight around her and crossed her arms to keep it closed. "What now?"

"Now we head back to town and go our separate ways." If Kendall had dated a lot, then she couldn't be innocent about how she was making him feel and think right now. She'd chosen that outfit knowing she was attractive in it. Knowing he'd have a hard time not being interested in her after spending time alone together.

"Can I come over by the controls with you?"

"Suit yourself."

She followed him to the control area and leaned against the booth, watching him steer. If he had been in a better mood, he would have taught her how to handle the controls and let her steer it for a few minutes, but the evening was shaded by his thoughts now.

What type of woman was Kendall? Really? At times she seemed completely genuine and innocent, but then she told him she was a serial dater. What did a man do with that sort of information? He'd jumped at a business proposition without knowing her, and now his word bound him to hosting weekly cruises with her.

He could still say no to her dating service, but even now he knew he wouldn't. Oh, he'd like to. But he wasn't a fool. Kendall was right. People would pay good money to take their significant other out on a private cruise and eat dinner under the stars. In the summer, he might be able to make more off that type of a business than he did from his shipments. Which really scraped his nerves.

They docked the boat and tied it up. He meant for them to part ways at that point, but Kendall hung around and waited for him to close everything down.

"Need any help?" she called from the pier.

"I'm good. You can hang on to my coat and give it back some other time if you want to head out."

"I'll wait for you."

Brice stopped stalling and finished by locking the

boat. He jumped to the pier and fell into step with Kendall.

Kendall bumped her shoulder into him, playfully. "Thanks for taking me out tonight. That was really beautiful. I feel like—" She froze in place and it took Brice a second to stop walking and turn back toward her to see why she'd stopped. Kendall's face contorted as if she was in pain.

Brice forgot that he wasn't going to get close to her and rushed back to her side, grabbing her elbows. "What's wrong?"

Her nostrils flared as she sucked in two deep breaths. Then she locked eyes with him. "Will you hold my hand and not let go, even if things get weird?"

"Weird?"

"Will you?"

"Yes." He offered his hand. She slipped hers into his and they laced their fingers together as if they'd been holding hands that way for years. Her hand was shaking. Hard.

He gave her a reassuring squeeze as his mind spun trying to think of a medical condition she could have. "You can trust me. If you want to tell me what's wrong, I'll listen."

Kendall cleared her throat. "I saw you duck behind that boat at the end of the pier. You might as well come out now."

Whom was she talking to?

Brice pulled Kendall up short. Goose Harbor was normally a very safe place, but crime wasn't known to spare any town. If someone lurked nearby, why hadn't she alerted him right away? Brice moved so he was angled a bit in front of Kendall.

A petite woman stepped out of the shadows. "I see you wasted no time finding a new man to cling to. How long will this one stick with you, Kenny? I'm thinking he looks like a runner with maybe a week or two in him max. Mark my words—he won't stick with you for long."

Brice volleyed his gaze between the two women. "Who—"

Kendall tightened her hold on his hand. "What do you want, Mom?"

Well, she sure hadn't lied about things getting weird.

Chapter Three

Kendall clenched her teeth and tried to calm down. *One. Two. Three.* She let air hiss out of her mouth slowly.

Her mother never responded to subtle hints, only clear, to-the-point statements. But Kendall wanted to be careful what she said in front of Brice because he hardly knew her. She didn't want him to judge her harshly based on this interaction. The adult child and parent relationship was a difficult one to navigate. She knew she needed to respect and honor her mother, but that didn't mean obeying her any longer. Especially when her mother's moral code was so different than Kendall's own. But what did that all look like when acted out in real life? It was hard to know. Especially with an emotionally imbalanced mother thrown into the mix.

Mom staggered forward a few feet. Drunk. "I need some money. As much as you can spare." Her words slurred a bit. "You'll help your mom out, won't you?"

A big part of Kendall's reason for leaving Kentucky had been to get away from her mother. The woman had been a constant drain on Kendall's savings, even after Kendall moved out of their trailer as a teenager. Not to mention the number of times her mother had stumbled into the country club, causing trouble for her. How had Mom found her so quickly? Kendall had left Kentucky without a trace. No forwarding address. No friends to leave information with. Had Mom followed her from the get-go and hung back, waiting until just the right moment? Well, what a moment to pick. Embarrassing her in front of her new friend while they were trying to plan a business venture together. He'd probably back out now, and Kendall couldn't blame him.

Still, she dug her nails into the back of Brice's hand. Poor man. "You need to go back home. I don't have any money to spare." Brice probably thought she was being a mean person, sending her mother away. If only he knew everything that had led up to this moment, maybe he'd understand. Maybe he'd take her side.

As if he could read her mind, Brice offered her hand an encouraging squeeze. At the touch, something inside her stomach unknotted. Kendall straightened her spine.

"No money to spare?" Her mother's eyebrows arched. "I've got to say, I don't know if I believe you, Kenny."

"I'm not sure how you found me, but you need to go back home. I have to start fresh here. Don't you see that?" Kendall pleaded. "It's my only chance."

"If you don't have money, then you must be getting it from somewhere—or someone—else. Is this the man paying your bills?" She pointed at Brice. "He won't keep you long. You realize that, don't you? I can see now he's too good for you. He'll tire of you quickly. Like they all do."

The muscles in Brice's arm coiled. Was he offended? More than likely, he was angry at Kendall for forcing him to be a part of this conversation.

Kendall's throat clamped up. While she didn't put much stock in anything her mom said, the woman knew exactly where to place a jab. But she knew better than to take Mom's words too much to heart. How could a daughter have faith in a parent who couldn't ever find money to pay the electric bills but had found plenty to purchase Gucci handbags and Christian Louboutin shoes and go on beachside vacations while her child sat at home shivering because unpaid bills had let the heat get cut off?

Kendall shook her thoughts from the past away. Revisiting negative memories from her childhood was like taking swigs of slow-burning poison—stupid and damaging. Besides, Mom was all she had. The woman might have been a terrible mother, but she had stayed. That was more than could be said for her father.

She opened her mouth, planning to relent and offer her mother a few hundred dollars if she promised not to come back to Goose Harbor, but Brice cleared his throat, stopping her.

"Ma'am, I mean no disrespect cutting into the conversation this way, but I think you've said enough. Kendall has stated her mind, so there isn't much left to do but go our separate ways."

Her mother rounded on him. "Are you the one giving her money? How is she starting a business? I had the log-ins to all of her accounts and I know she doesn't have a nest egg that large anywhere."

"Mom!" Kendall fisted her hands. Her mother had promised to stop trying to get into her accounts, but

Kendall should have known better. With a long string of criminal-minded friends, Mom always had someone willing to help her…for a price. If her mother had figured out her new passwords, then that explained how she'd located her in Goose Harbor. It also made her incredibly dangerous to have around. Did she know the password to Kendall's email account, as well? Fear seized her heart, causing her muscles to freeze. What if her mother knew about Sesser Atwood? She could ruin everything before Kendall even had an opportunity to succeed.

She thought back over the meeting with Sesser and Claire. How had they explained the final term of the contract? Should the partnership become public, Mr. Atwood had the right to back out of his deal with her and call in her loan in full.

Thinking of the loan, plus the cost of the furniture in her office and everything else Sesser had given her, Kendall swallowed hard. It would take her years and a lot of hard work and sacrifice to pay the loan back if he called it in. More important, she'd lose her business—her dream.

Brice angled his body in front of her in a protective way. "Like I said, it's best if you leave."

Her mother peeked around him to make eye contact. "Looks like you found a dog with some bark this time. But we both know he won't last. Not with you. You're too much like me, Kenny. Neither of us can keep a man. That's why we need each other." She gave a small wave and headed back down the pier. "I'll see you later."

Brice held on to Kendall's hand while her mother staggered across the beach. His eyes never left her, as if he was on high alert. Neither of them said a word, even after her mother disappeared from view.

Finally Kendall broke contact and dropped her head into her hands, grabbing fistfuls of hair. "I'm so sorry you had to hear all that. What must you think of me?"

"I'm not sorry." Brice placed his hands on her upper arms, getting her to meet his eyes again. "I'm glad I was here…glad she listened. Here's hoping I'm around next time she shows up too."

"I don't think she would have left so easily if I had been alone."

His eyebrows formed a V. "Is she always like that?"

"Sometimes worse." Kendall tried to offer a smile but failed miserably. "You must think I'm a horrible person, speaking to my own mother like that and telling her I won't help her."

He let go of her and blew out a long stream of air. "Believe me, you couldn't be more wrong. My own family…" He turned away and scanned the boatyard before turning his attention back to her. "How she speaks to you… It's not kind."

"You get used to it." Kendall pulled his coat tighter around her middle.

"You shouldn't have to."

She shrugged. "I tried to leave without letting her know where I was going so I could get a clean start away from her. You see how well that went." She gathered her hair in one hand, catching it all at the nape of her neck so it would stop whipping into her face.

"What are you going to do?"

"What can I do?" She let her hair go so she could toss up her hands. "She's my mom."

Brice steepled his fingers and pressed the tips to his

lips for a moment, thinking. "My father isn't the best man. He has a pretty bad reputation in town. If you stick around long enough, I'm sure you'll hear about him sooner or later." He shoved his hands deep into his pockets. "All that to say, we don't get to choose our family, but we can choose how we let them affect us. We choose the type of power they have over us."

"Easy for you to say. It looks like you have more than just your dad." An image of Evan and Brice hunched over the wood carving together projected onto her mind. "For me? It's only the two of us. I get her or I get no one. Not the best set of options if you ask me."

Brice's lips tugged with a sad smile of understanding. "Anyway, if you ever want to talk about it… I'm around and I'm willing to listen."

"I'll try to remember that."

Brice watched Kendall like a hawk the whole time they were talking. He'd misjudged her yesterday. Completely. He'd pegged her as a cheerful woman without a care in the world. What other type would start a date-planning service?

But he'd been wrong.

A quote the new young pastor at the church was fond of repeating filtered back into his mind. Something about being kind to every person because there was always something going on in everyone's life—a battle—that the outsider looking in may never even know about. Kendall proved that. The beautiful woman Brice met yesterday hid a lifetime of emotional scars delivered by one of the people a daughter should have been most able to trust.

Not unlike his own upbringing.

Brice touched the scar on his cheek. "Will she follow you home? Will you be safe on your own?"

"She'd never actually hurt me." Kendall started down the pier and reached the landing. A cool summer breeze whistled in between the boats in the harbor, causing some of them to bob back and forth. Masts with bells jingled.

Brice trailed her. "Words count as hurting."

"I can handle her."

It didn't look like it. He bit back the words he wanted to say. If he'd read Kendall correctly, she'd been seconds from caving to her mother's demands for money before he stepped in. Her mother would approach her again. Then what? But they didn't know each other well enough for him to press the point, so he dropped it.

Besides, he was one to talk. How much money had he given his father over the years just to keep the peace? He knew full well all that money ended up being used to gamble on the riverboats and not on food or items for the house as his dad had promised. Just like the money Dad had demanded in the latest voice mail. But his parents still had Laura in the house to take care of. Brice was never able to say no when his father dropped his sister's name and said she needed something. So foolishly, until last year when Laura became old enough to have her own cell phone when Brice could call and check in on her, he'd still been handing over a lot of money to his parents.

Technically he was the worst person imaginable to advise Kendall on dealing with her mother. It would be best if they steered clear of family conversations going forward.

He fell into step beside Kendall. "Let me at least walk you back to your car. Where'd you park?"

"Next to that warehouse." She pointed.

Brandon Hankman's warehouse? Oh no. In Hankman's world there was only black and white—no gray. If someone broke a rule, he was sure to point it out and want to see them pay a penalty.

Brice's gut twisted. "Not in a spot?"

"I wasn't able to find any spots…" Kendall's words faltered as they rounded the warehouse. She froze. "Where's my car? It was right here." She grabbed his arm and jiggled it as if he'd been the one to move her vehicle. "Where'd it go? My mother—"

"She probably has nothing to do with this." But Hankman no doubt did. "It's been towed."

Her eyebrows shot up into her bangs. "Towed?"

"And you won't be able to get it until Monday. The city's lot is only open during business hours."

"Until Monday?" Her voice got higher. "What kind of town is this?"

"A small one that can't staff the lot on the weekends."

"Maybe these are all signs. What if my business is doomed to fail? I should never have tried to make all this happen." She looked as if she might start crying.

Brice's stomach twisted into a knot. If there was one thing he was even worse at handling than parental relationships, it was crying women. *Please don't cry. Help. How can I encourage her?*

That thought shocked him. Usually Brice was introverted, but something about Kendall put him at ease. Perhaps it was her open way of talking. Whatever it was, if he thought about it any more he'd clam up.

His favorite verse instantly came to mind. "Now, don't talk like that." He offered her what he hoped was an encouraging smile. "God doesn't give us a spirit of fear. That discouragement isn't coming from Him, so toss it away. God gives us strength and…" What was the rest of that verse? "God doesn't want you giving up on a dream He's given you."

"Do you really believe God cares about our dreams?"

"I'd like to believe He does." Brice motioned for her to follow him. "My car's by my building. I'll drive you home."

His shipping business was located two buildings down. He should have given her the address and explained where to park when she called earlier, but phone conversations made him uncomfortable and he always tried to end them as quickly as he could. "From now on, when we do these sunset cruises or if you need to come down to the docks for any reason, you can park by my warehouse and your car will be fine there."

She bumped her shoulder into his. "So, after everything, you still want to go on this adventure with me?"

Adventure? The word pulled at something deep in his gut.

It had been a long time since he'd had one of those.

Brice couldn't help the smile that crept across his face. "You can't get rid of me that easily."

"I'm glad to hear it."

While he wasn't overly thrilled about the idea of being a part of a date-planning service, he was smart enough to admit that he needed the money that it could potentially bring in. And if he was being honest, Kendall intrigued him, and he wasn't going to turn down the opportunity to spend time with her every week. A woman like Kendall would be sought after once some of the other bachelors in Goose Harbor discovered her. He'd lose her undivided attention quickly, but Brice could enjoy her company while it lasted.

His hand closed around his car keys, letting the metal bite into his palm.

This wasn't like him at all—entertaining daydreams of spending time with a woman he hardly knew. No... make that spending time with any woman at all. He'd set the desire for a wife and family to the side. He had his shipping business to worry about, his little sister to watch over, but most important, he'd decided ten years ago that relationships weren't for him.

A man tended to think like that after the woman he was dating responded to his marriage proposal by laughing right in his face.

He shook his head.

Maybe he was overtired or stressed. Brice rubbed his jaw. He hadn't been sleeping well. That had to be it. Because it couldn't be that he was attracted to Kendall. That didn't fit into the plan he had for his life. Not one bit.

Chapter Four

"I'll check into the hot air balloon idea, but I don't think that'll be a problem." Kendall smiled as she spoke into the phone because she'd learned early on in her event-planning career that doing so made her voice stay pleasant despite her stress level. The man on the other end of the line was planning how to propose to his girlfriend; of course Kendall would do everything she could to make the date perfect.

"Great. Do you know when you'll be able to call me with a ballpark figure?"

"By Monday at the latest." Kendall wrote a note in her planner along with the man's phone number.

"That'll work."

"She's blessed to have you." She turned toward her computer and opened a new web browser. "You sound very thoughtful."

"Not as blessed as I am to have her."

The bell that hung above the door to her building rang as Kendall ended the phone call, but she turned away from the entrance, back to her computer, determined to find a good deal for the hot air balloon date.

So far, yesterday and all of today, not once had the creaking front door meant someone was entering her portion of the divided building. Although a very steady line of customers—mostly women—entered Evan's woodshop.

Brice's younger brother definitely had the charm of the family. Kendall fought an eye roll. She'd experienced the attention of enough *charming* men to last a lifetime. No, thank you. Her past showed that men like Evan only stayed interested in a woman until the next one walked by. Attention was nice, but it didn't last. If she had to describe the man of her dreams—which of course she wasn't looking for because she wasn't interested in dating—these days Kendall preferred men like Brice. Steady, dependable and—

"Well, don't you just look all in a daze?" The singsong voice of Claire Atwood broke through Kendall's thoughts.

"Claire." Kendall jolted from her seat, upending her foam coffee cup. Her mocha spattered over the edge of the desk and cascaded onto the floor with a splash. A small *eep!* escaped from Claire's lips as she dodged the liquid, narrowly missing getting some on her white pants.

"Oh no." Kendall raced to the back room and returned with a wad of paper towels. "I know there's a bell on my door, but I didn't hear you. I'm so sorry." She dabbed at the spilled coffee, catching most of it before it rolled toward the computer tower. Her day planner, on the other hand, was completely soaked. Ruined.

Sesser's daughter sprang into action. She ran back for more paper towels and then bent down to mop up the rest of the mess from the floor. "You didn't hear me? I don't know how that could be possible! We'll have to get you a bigger bell over the door." She laughed.

"Please don't." Kendall shoved all the dripping towels into the waste bin. She'd deal with emptying the now-jammed trash can later. "You and your father have already done so much for me. I can't accept any more. I can't—"

"How about one more tiny, little thing?" Claire held up a manicured nail and winked at her.

"I couldn't pos—"

"But first, care if I close the door?" Claire padded across the office on ballet flats and shut the front door.

The woman was everything Kendall wasn't—poised, tall and slender—beautiful with pale skin and reddish copper hair. Even in four-inch heels, Kendall wouldn't have been eye level with her.

"Here." Claire walked back to Kendall's desk and placed a business card in front of her in the same manner as if she was handing over a trophy. "He's going to call you for an interview probably in the next day or two, so if you want to work through some quotable material, I'm game."

Kendall picked up the card. *Jason Moss. Reporter.* "An interview?"

Claire nodded. "He's the editor of the local paper, but his pieces often get picked up by the bigger papers and news outlets, and he's a part of a tourist-friendly blog too. The initial publicity will be great, and if it gets picked up, that could mean big business for you."

"It's all a bit overwhelming." Kendall still had dates to research, another client to call back and a meeting with Brice in the morning to help paint the boat they would use for the sunset cruises. Her business had been open for only two days. How would she manage more? "I don't know what to say. Thank you."

"Remember not to mention the partnership with my father, though." Claire tilted her head and spoke in a whisper. "If it becomes public, he has the right to back out of his deal with you and call in your loan in full. Remember that."

A rumble of dread simmered low in Kendall's chest. "I'm aware of that." She pressed a pushpin through the business card and stuck it onto the corkboard wall behind her computer. "I won't say a thing."

Claire sank into the chair on the other side of the desk and dropped her large purse into her lap. "Speaking of Daddy, he mentioned that you've already set up a weekly event. Way to make quick work of that." She winked. "I'm so impressed."

Kendall folded her hands on top of the bare desk, missing her day planner already. "Brice Daniels and I are going to host weekly sunset cruises and have even talked about expanding to dinner tours if the cruises go well."

"Oh." Claire's smile faltered. "One of the Daniels boys. I see."

Kendall licked her lips. "Do you know him?"

"Of course." Her smile came back, but it pulled tight around the corners. Forced. "It's my family's business to know everyone in town."

"But…do you like him?" Why was Kendall's heart pounding so hard?

"Honestly I'm not close to Brice Daniels, but I've had…dealings with other people in his family." Claire's gaze skirted toward the wall that separated Kendall's office from Evan's storefront. "Let's just say they didn't prove to be dependable." She closed her eyes tightly for a moment. "But we're talking business, not gossiping about Goose Harbor locals, right?"

"Of course."

"My father thinks you have a great idea, and he's excited to be a part of it. I just stopped by to see if you needed help with anything else."

"Excited?" The man had not seemed thrilled when she last talked to him. Pleased maybe—at the opportunity to diversify his business dealings—but not excited.

"Well, as excited as my dad gets." Claire grinned. "He has a pretty monotone emotional scale, so don't take any offense if he acts like being your partner is as fun as eating broccoli."

"Good to know."

"Besides, you'll deal with me and not him most of the time." Claire laid her hand over her heart. A gold watch with diamonds around the face let Kendall know that while Claire might joke about her father's monotone emotions, she was a daddy's girl. Or at the least, didn't mind spending her father's money.

She pulled a piece of paper from her purse. "In that vein, here are some numbers you can reach me at." Claire handed over the paper—home, parents' home, cell and office. At the bottom of the page was written GHonaDime4.

Claire kept speaking. "You can call me at any time if you have questions or concerns." Her eyes widened, as if she had remembered something. "While we're talking business, you should know that we've set up a professional website for you. I'm managing it for now, so let me know if there is anything you want changed or updated. The password is at the bottom of the page so you can go on and add things and we can link your social media so you can have a live stream of pictures and Tweets for advertising."

Password. So that explained the odd word on the page.

"A website?" Kendall set the paper down and rubbed her temples. While the Atwoods' enthusiasm was encouraging, it was a lot to take in all at once. Kendall couldn't help dwelling for a second on the fact that most of her business decisions had been taken away in the deal. What if she'd wanted to plan her own website?

"We want you to be successful, and we're here to make sure that happens. But, Kendall…" Claire smiled again. "We're not here to steamroll you or your dream. Got that? At least I'm not. I'm going to be a middleman between you and my father, but I'd also like to be your friend. Those phone numbers I gave you… You can call me for things other than business. Actually I'd like that a lot."

Kendall nodded but wondered about the wisdom of becoming friends with the daughter of someone she'd gone into business with. Claire seemed nice enough, though, and the guarded look in her large blue eyes made Kendall wonder if—just maybe—it was lonely being the only daughter of a wealthy, powerful businessman. And if anyone knew about feeling alone, it was no-roots-in-life Kendall. Her heart went out to the woman.

"I'd like that too."

Claire let out a breath. "Now that all of that is settled, I have to head out. More meetings. You know how that goes." She pulled her phone out of her purse, glanced at it and put it back. "I'll see you around."

On the way out, Claire closed the door again. Kendall glanced at the clock and discovered it was past time to lock up. She might as well close up the shop and head home, where she could work on her laptop in the comfort of her sweatpants.

A light knock sounded at the door just as she was gathering the plastic bag out of the waste bin. Who— besides Claire—would stop in so late?

"Come in?" she called with a slight amount of hesitation.

Brice's brother ducked his head inside the door. "I'm not interrupting you, am I?"

She shoved her thick bangs out of the way of her eyes as she stood. "How can I help you, Evan?"

"Oh…nothing… I just thought…" He wrapped his hand over the back of his neck. "Did I see…? Was that Claire Atwood in here a few minutes ago?"

"It was." Kendall tied the top end of the garbage bag in a knot and then looked back over at him again. "Did you need something else?"

"No." He shrugged but stayed in the same spot. "Was she here to have a date planned?"

If Kendall answered honestly, that could lead to more questions, but she also didn't want to lie. It was clear by how they both behaved that something obviously had happened between Evan and Claire in the past, so no matter what she said, she also didn't want to make him believe something incorrect either.

Kendall shoved a file folder into her large purse. "She was only here as a friend."

"Right. Of course. I should have…" Evan grabbed the door handle. "Have a great night, okay?"

"You too." Kendall waved as he shut the door.

She shook her head and bit back an exasperated laugh. At least she could say one thing for the Daniels brothers. They knew how to keep a girl on her toes. It was clear whom Evan cared about. If only Brice was as easy to read.

Taking a deep breath, Brice filled his lungs with the smell of sawdust and new plastic—common, working-man smells. That simple practice helped ease the knot in his gut that had been there since leaving his second voice mail at Sesser Atwood's office.

Couldn't the man return a phone call?

Brice half believed that Sesser wasn't returning his messages simply because he was one of the Danielses and Atwood and Brice's father had an ocean full of bad water under their bridge. Truth be known, they hadn't even built a bridge over the gulf between the families. Nothing could. Still, for the sunset cruises he needed to move his paddle wheeler to the downtown pier. Kendall was right. Tourists only showed up on the working dock if they were lost and looking for directions. They never came there by choice. But he couldn't arrange to have a sunset cruise boat at the correct pier if Sesser wouldn't return his calls, which meant he'd have to go speak to the man in person.

Brice gulped in another huge breath of sawdust air.

He pushed the large shopping cart down the aisle of the hardware store toward the outdoor paints while Kendall lagged behind. With her attention trained on her smartphone and not on where she was going, she'd bumped into him at least three times. He'd already saved her from knocking over a huge display of motor oil.

He turned a corner and waited to make sure she didn't get lost. A teenage boy cut close in front of her, almost making her lose her footing. For a moment, her large eyes went even wider. She lost hold of her cell phone but then flung out her arm, catching it against her stomach as she stumbled forward.

Brice grabbed her elbow, steadying her. "You know, if you put that thing down and watched where you were going, you wouldn't keep almost falling."

Kendall swiped a notification off the screen. "Right." She didn't look up. "I'd also have to wait to respond to this email, which would cost me time that I need to use to call vendors later. Time is money. You've heard that expression before, haven't you?" Her gaze bounced up to his for a heartbeat.

"Sure." He gently covered her phone's screen with his hand. "But how about the one that says turn off the phone and live your life?"

She narrowed her eyes as a small smile crept onto her face. "That doesn't sound like a famous saying."

"It's not, but it should be."

She tugged the phone out from under his hand and started typing on it again. "I have four dates to plan and it's only opening week. Can you believe that? I envisioned this all starting slower."

"Too much business? Sounds like a good problem to have." He wished he had such a *problem*. Not that he could complain. God always took care of his needs, but sometimes—especially lately—it felt like he and

God were in different time zones altogether. Their timing never quite lined up.

Yesterday there hadn't been enough money to pay his men, cover the insurance costs on all his boats, fully gas them and do all the required repairs. And if there was one thing he'd never do, it was shortchange his workers. So they'd shuffled shipments around, combining the goods based on drop-off locations so they could use fewer boats, pulling ones out of dock that weren't going to be insured that month. His company would receive payment upon delivery and Brice would be in the black again—but for how long? He'd worried. Paced his tin-can-sized office in the warehouse. And prayed.

Before he'd finished praying, Tony Castillo, who owned Castillo's Carrying, Brice's biggest competitor, had contacted him, offering Brice one of his big shipments. Castillo's barge was broken and the goods needed to get to Chicago in a hurry. The payment Tony quoted was better than anything that had come Brice's way in months, so of course he accepted it. He and his crew had scrambled to move around the shipments again to accommodate the job he'd taken from Castillo, and thankfully they'd made it out of dock just in time. As much as he respected Tony Castillo and didn't want to take work away from the man, with Atwood raising the docking prices again, Brice could use the extra business. Desperately.

God had taken care of his needs. Like always. But… why couldn't it happen a day or two before Brice was at the edge of despairing?

Brice stopped walking and Kendall ran right into his back. He turned around and crossed his arms. "If you've got things to do, I can drive you back to your office and I'll paint the boat on my own. I don't mind."

"No." She finally stowed her cell phone in her back pocket. "I got you into the cruising business, so I'll help make it ready."

"The boat needed work either way."

"Still." She mimicked his pose. "I told you I'd help."

"Listen. I'm offering an out if you want it."

Kendall tilted her head, considering him for a moment. "I don't."

"You sure?" He fought a smile. Her determination amid her obvious stress was cute.

She lifted her chin. "Positive."

"All right, then." He pushed the cart until they were next to the large tubs of paint suitable for using on the paddle wheeler.

The first sunset cruise was scheduled for Friday, leaving them only four more days to finish getting the boat into shape. He'd yet to iron out a deal with Sesser for a dock at the downtown pier, but they didn't want to hold up operations waiting on that.

"Which color do you think we should use?" Brice looked over his shoulder to meet Kendall's gaze. She seemed distracted this morning, her deep brown eyes full of emotion. He sensed her mood went beyond her stress. "Hey." He dipped his head a little to be right on her level. "Are you okay?"

"I'm fine." Her smile looked forced. "Just distracted, is all. I never realized how much I'd have to accomplish every day to run a business."

"It never really ends." If he didn't write down every little thing, he'd lose track of the repairs his boats needed each week. But she didn't need to hear about how busy or stressed he was. Biting her lip, Kendall looked just as breakable as she had the night her mom showed up on the pier. A need to protect her filled his chest with so much force he took a step back, making the cart bump against the metal shelving with a loud *clang*. Where had that come from? The urge to protect wasn't foreign, but it usually only came around with such ferocity when his siblings were in danger.

Brice shook his head. He only felt that way because she was so petite and she'd confided to him that she didn't have any friends in town. And yes, he liked her smile and her laugh and the way she made him forget that he usually had a hard time talking to people.

He took another deep breath of the comforting warehouse air and then swallowed hard. "You'll do great."

"I hope so." Her tentative smile made his stomach kick. "Thank you, you know, for believing in me."

"Know what? This paint will work." He grabbed the first one he saw, heaved it into the cart and steered toward the checkout lanes as if he and Kendall were playing tag and he needed to run away from her.

Maybe they were, but he couldn't let her catch him. The situation with Audra had taught him that once he fell for someone, he fell hard. And Brice was done falling.

Chapter Five

Paintbrush in hand, Kendall jogged over to the old-school boom box in Brice's warehouse and turned the music up. Dust motes trailed through the air in her wake. He'd left the building's huge rolling front doors open, so sunlight streamed in and a gentle but steady breeze wrapped them in air carrying a mix of fresh-caught fish, dampness from the lake, something frying at the nearest restaurant and oil. To her surprise, Kendall discovered the eclectic smell didn't bother her.

When they returned from the hardware store, his men had already moved the paddle wheeler inside to what Brice called a dry dock, which Kendall realized was exactly that. The boat was hoisted in the air inside the building so people could work on every inch of it and the paint on the bottom could dry. To her disappointment, Brice's crew had disassembled the paddles and repainted them the day before. She'd been looking forward to splashing them with bright red. Instead she and Brice were working on covering the bottom and lower sides in a respectable gleaming white. Boring.

But he promised her they'd paint the top half a deep hunter green, so that had to count for something.

She fast-stepped to the beat back toward the boat and dipped her brush in the tub of paint on her way. "Don't you love this song?" she hollered to Brice as she applied a liberal amount of the white to the boat's side.

Brice had been quiet on the way back from the hardware store, which wasn't abnormal for him. In the past week she'd noticed that he tended to stay silent unless he had something important to say, but silence with Brice never felt awkward. Which was strange considering Kendall's normal propensity for filling every moment with conversation, but somehow Brice's desire to only speak words that mattered soothed her. She didn't feel pressure to say something entertaining or try to dazzle him. She could simply relax and be herself—a person she was only beginning to realize loved quiet and comfortable silence with another person.

He chuckled from his crouched position under the boat. "I can't say that I know it. But no one's ever accused me of being a music buff." In his backward baseball hat, button-down shirt with the sleeves rolled up and well-worn jeans, the man fit his environment perfectly.

"Don't know it?" She dropped her hand holding the brush so it rested on her side and then turned and gaped at him. "But this one's been on the radio basically on repeat for the past two months."

"Sorry to disappoint." He shrugged and got to his feet.

She popped her hands to her hips. "Top five songs on your MP3 player?"

"Don't own one."

"You're a rare man, Brice Daniels."

"Is that a good rare or a 'send this back to the kitchen to get cooked better' rare?"

"I wouldn't send you back." She winked and then a tinge of embarrassment flushed her cheeks. She hadn't flirted that openly in a long time. And she really should stop. Teasing a man usually led to a date, and a few of those led to getting to know him more and then having to cut and run before the man realized she wasn't worth sticking around for. Really, all her ex-boyfriends should thank her. She'd saved them time in the end. They wouldn't have wanted to stick with her. No man did.

Stepping past her, Brice made his way to the paint tray and set his brush down. On his way back, he paused near her and Kendall looked up at his face. Wow. The man had such pretty eyes. They were an intense pale green. So similar to the underside of a leaf. Her fingers itched to touch the scar on his cheek, but she shook that thought away. Where had it even come from?

"Want to take a break?" He leaned close to her ear so she could hear him over the radio.

Her pulse thumbed hard against her veins. Maybe a reaction to the loud music? She took a step back and nodded.

He tossed her a rag and began wiping off his hands with another one before he motioned her to follow him. Along the far wall of the warehouse, at the top of a set of metal stairs, Brice held open a door that led to a small office. It was sparse. Basically only what needed to be there was there. An aged and worn desk, a lamp, two faded chairs. No knickknacks. A single, thriving plant near the bank of windows was the only thing about the room that didn't look straight from a furniture store's back discount room.

He reached into a cube fridge hidden in the closet and tossed her a bottle of water. "Catch."

She caught it, twisted off the cap and gulped down a third of the bottle. Replacing the cap, she used the back of her hand to swipe at her mouth. A muscle in her arm pinched, making her wince. "Wow. All this bending and reaching." She stretched her arms into the air, trying to figure out where she was the sorest. "It's working some muscles I didn't realize I even had."

Bottle in hand, he watched her, smiling.

Nerves blossomed in her stomach under his inspection; she twisted the bottle around in her hands and then plopped into a nearby chair, which groaned in retaliation. "I saw your brother Evan last night."

Brice quirked his eyebrows. "Has his woodworking been bothering you still? I could talk to him for—"

"It's not like that at all. He's fine. I just…" She looked down at the floor. Why had she started this conversation? Now she'd have to finish, or think of something to say, because the way Brice was leaning forward with his eyebrows raised left little room for anything else. She sucked in some lake-tinged air. "Did something happen between your brother and Claire Atwood?"

He fumbled his water bottle before setting it onto his desk. "What makes you ask?"

"No real reason." Besides the strange way they both acted yesterday.

Brice lowered himself into his desk chair. He leaned back, the metal squeaking. "Are you interested in Evan?"

"Oh no." She shook her head. "It's not like that at all."

"Because if you are…" He adjusted his seat to lean forward. "I'm going to tell you right now that he's not interested."

"Brice!" She dropped the lid to the water bottle. It bounced on the floor before rolling into Brice's shoe. "I didn't mean it like that."

"Then why did you ask?" He rested his elbows onto his desk. "When we first met, you told me you dated a lot. Evan's my little brother and—"

"In the past, yes, I have." Why was he even bringing that up? She should never have told him about her past. Now Brice thought she had her cap set on his brother and of course he was going to try to save Evan from the woman he considered a serial dater. After the nice time they'd spent together, Brice thought she was capable of using his brother? That hurt. "But that's not who I am any longer and that's not what this is about."

"What happened in your relationships?" He pursed his lips before adding, "Why didn't any of them stick?"

Mental note: don't prod Brice for answers, because he only comes back with even tougher questions.

Kendall worked her jaw back and forth. How much should she tell him? "If you have to know, I've always been the one to break up with the guy. It just…" She shrugged and looked away.

"Just what?"

Fine. She'd give him the truth, because then everything would be out in the open and he'd know that she was only interested in friendship with both him and his brother. Saying something painful now would alleviate the need for an awkward conversation later—

the conversation that eventually happened anytime she pursued a friendship with a man. The one where they tried to veer things onto a romantic path, a path she couldn't walk with a man on, no matter how much she wanted to.

"I think I always wanted to see if I was worth fighting to keep." She stared down at where her fingers laced together and then added in a small voice, "Apparently I'm not." Tears burned against her eyes, begging to be released. She swiped at her face, trying to compose herself.

When she met his gaze again, Brice was studying her in an open way.

Why had she phrased her answer that way? Now he pitied her and she didn't want that. She'd only wanted him to know that she was damaged goods when it came to relationships. To shut the door on any possibility of something growing between them that she'd never be able to follow through on. And she needed to, because she already felt a pull toward him…a desire to get to know him more and spend time with him. But if he pursued her, she'd wind up hurting him or breaking up with him when the relationship started to feel too real—too lasting. She'd run before he could.

Evidently she was like her father that way. The realization stung.

Brice rubbed his jaw. "Ken—"

His phone interrupted whatever he was going to say. Instead of picking it up, Brice glared at his telephone as if it were a monster in need of slaying.

"I can leave if you want to answer that." Kendall grabbed her water bottle and started to stand.

Brice motioned for her to sit back down and then he

snagged the receiver and answered the phone. After only a minute he swiveled his chair so his back was facing her. The phone cord wrapped around his side as it pulled taut.

"What? I have a hard time believing— You can't do this to us. You can't keep squeezing the last penny out of every person who rents at your dock. Someday you'll have competition. Someday—" Brice scrubbed his hand down his face, turned around and slammed the phone back down.

"Bad news?" Kendall offered an apologetic smile.

His gaze bounced back to her and he schooled his expression, dropping the snarl that had pulled at his lips so his mouth relaxed. "How do you even know the Atwoods?"

Oh. So he was launching right back into their conversation about Evan. She didn't want to lie but also couldn't share about her partnership—the whole reason she knew Claire. "Claire stopped by Love on a Dime the other day."

"Of course she did." Brice snorted. "Right in front of Evan."

Okay, this line of conversation was going nowhere fast. *For future reference, don't ask Brice about Evan. It doesn't go well.*

Redirect him. "Are you having problems with the dockyard?"

He laced his fingers together and put them behind his head. "He's jacked up the prices again. How does he expect any of us to make a living if he keeps finding loopholes in the contract so he can up our fees?"

Kendall twisted the water bottle around and around in her hands as she spoke. "If you don't like the terms for this dock, can you move your boats somewhere else?"

"Not if I want to stay in Goose Harbor." He dropped his hands to his sides, and his shoulders slumped. "He owns all the docks."

"All the docks?" She leaned back in her chair and crossed her arms. "I find that hard to believe. There are docks all along the shoreline."

"Private, residential docks, yes. But I can't work out of those. There are laws and codes that have to be followed. Besides, none of those docks are dug deep enough for these bigger ships."

That made sense. "I guess I don't know a lot about shipping."

He tugged off his baseball hat and ran his fingers over his close-cropped hair. "If I had my way and enough money, I'd petition the city board for the right to dig another dock and I'd charge better, fairer fees to anyone who wanted to dock their boats there."

"Then why don't you?"

"Like I said, money. But these cruise tours are going to help. I have a good feeling about them." He used his baseball hat to point at her. "You just might be the key to reaching my dream."

Kendall's breath caught. He was only talking about his desire to build an additional pier, but still, warmth curled in her chest at the thought of being a vital piece to anyone's dreams.

Seated behind the steering wheel of the freshly painted paddle wheeler, Brice watched as Kendall ushered in the guests for their first-ever sunset cruise.

She'd asked him to dress nice, so he'd worn a starched button-up with his least-worn-out pair of jeans and the leather shoes he usually reserved for church. He'd even cracked open the hairstyling gel his sister had given him last Christmas. When he left his cabin, he'd thought he fit what Kendall wanted.

Then he saw Kendall.

On clicking heels she seemed to all but float from guest to guest, complimenting them and making sure they were comfortable before the boat left port. Her hair was curled in a way that made her look like a movie star, and she wore a black dress that whispered back and forth against her knees as she walked. Dangling bracelets and a long necklace completed her look, but she hadn't needed the adornments to catch his eye. Brice could hardly look away.

Earlier in the day they'd met and he'd set up chairs and a food table while Kendall hung paper lanterns from the ceiling and arranged flowers on smaller tables that she deemed private sitting areas. She'd been in shorts and a T-shirt while they worked and he'd considered her beautiful then. Granted, she was the type of woman who would look beautiful in baggy sweatpants on a sick day. But she didn't act as if she knew how pretty she was. Perhaps she didn't realize it. Which only added to her appeal.

She stepped beside him, the hem of her dress brushing his leg as she leaned close and covered his hand with hers for the space of a heartbeat.

When his sister was younger, she used to love the cartoon princess movies and often begged her brothers to watch them with her. Brice had given in more often than Andrew and Evan had, so he knew all the stories by heart now. Brice's eyes met Kendall's deep brown ones. So this was how Prince Eric felt in his sister's favorite cartoon movie about the mermaid who turned into a woman? When Laura was little she used to dance around their house singing a song about kissing.

Kiss her. His mouth went dry.

"We're ready for liftoff." Kendall squeezed his hand and returned to their cruise guests.

He flexed his hand against the memory of heat in the place she had touched. *Focus.* He cleared his throat and started the paddle wheeler. Kendall picked up the mic. As the boat began to churn its way up the shoreline, she started to share historical facts.

"The Goose Harbor area was almost lost at the turn of the century because of the lumber boom. People didn't realize that by removing all the trees they were letting the dunes creep in and take over the town. A group of forward-thinking individuals formed the Society in Favor of Saving Goose Harbor and started a program to reforest the area and stop the movement of the dunes. Thanks to them, our town still stands and we can all enjoy this gorgeous view."

She pointed out the eagles and shared information about their conservation, and as they headed out farther onto the lake, she stunned Brice by launching into details about the active shipping industry on Lake Michigan. She had the gift of tilting her voice and sharing facts in such a way that made them all interesting, instead of how he would have said everything…like a boring history professor. Kendall must have spent a lot of time researching and learning about Goose Harbor to know all that. Did she already love this town and feel as tied to it as he was?

When the sun began to fall toward the horizon, he dropped the anchors so couples could stroll to the edge and wrap their arms around each other and watch the stunning display of nature. Kendall worked the crowd, handing out hors d'oeuvres and offering to snap pictures on people's cell phones. She'd been right about people taking selfies near the paddles. Once everyone seemed settled, she found an open spot at the railing and turned to watch the sunset.

Before he realized what he was doing, Brice's feet ate up the distance between the steering wheel and Kendall and he joined her. He wrapped his fingers around the cool metal of the railing and looked down at her, studying the play of orange and pink twilight on her features. Her gaze was fixed on the setting sun, her eyes wide and mouth slightly parted. She was beautiful, and for the first time since they'd begun this venture together, he wished he was one of the dummies on the date instead of on this side of things, running the event. If he'd brought Kendall, he'd have his arm around her right now. Know what it felt like to have her head resting against his shoulder.

He shook his thoughts away and moved to put space between them, but Kendall reached out and slipped her fingers over his wrist. "Stay."

He nodded and swallowed against the lump in his throat. What was he doing to himself? Kendall had made it clear that she didn't want a relationship with any man. She said she'd left dating in the past. He had too.

She turned toward him and whispered, "We did good, didn't we?" She added a wink and bumped his shoulder with hers.

"Better than good." His words came out hoarse.

"Here's to dreaming." She flashed him a smile before turning back to the guests and announcing that they'd head back to shore in five minutes.

He made his way to the steering wheel and started the engine again but kept his eyes on Kendall. "Here's to dreaming indeed."

Chapter Six

Kendall had to get ahold of Brice.

"Answer your phone," she pleaded into her receiver.

Six unanswered calls to the phone at his warehouse and ten more to his cell phone. She'd called it even though she knew he never took the phone off Silent. Still, shouldn't he check his messages after two hours? Glance at his phone once? Most men her age were glued to their smartphone screens whether it was playing a game, reading articles, following sports or catching up on social media. She saw it all the time at restaurants—two people on a date who were both attached to their phones the whole time. Perhaps Brice's aversion to phones had merit. Either way, at a time like this, it was still annoying.

Kendall pushed away from her desk, clicked off her computer and stuffed a stack of file folders into her top drawer. It was past seven in the evening and she should have left her storefront an hour ago. A loud bang next door let her know that she wasn't the only one working late tonight. Evan might know how to get ahold of Brice. It was worth a try.

She slipped out her front door and entered Evan's woodshop. Brice's brother must have heard her enter, because he looked her way.

"Evening, Kendall." He straightened from where he was working on a block of wood and pressed his hands into his lower back. "I'm just shaving this down. I hope it wasn't too loud."

"Not at all." She'd never live down the first time they met when she was grumpy with him about using the loud saw. "Actually I'm trying to track down Brice."

"He's not here." Evan glanced over his shoulder as if he might find Brice crouching in the corner of his store.

"Oh, I know." She let out a puff of air that ruffled her bangs. If she didn't locate Brice soon, she'd have to call back the owner of the nearby bed-and-breakfast, Kellen Ashby, and tell him she couldn't accommodate the date he wanted her to plan for the next evening. So she pressed on. "I've tried his phone a couple times, both his office and cell phone numbers, but I haven't gotten an answer."

"You probably won't." Evan dusted his hands off on his jeans. "Brice doesn't like talking on the phone."

"I need to get ahold of him, though—it's semiurgent."

"I'm sure he's at his house." He used his thumb to point over his shoulder.

Okay, Evan definitely was the type who needed a direct question asked. No dropping hints with this guy. "Could you possibly call Brice's house phone and tell him to call me?"

Evan grinned and shook his head. "Unfortunately my grizzly bear of a brother doesn't have a landline."

Yeah, Evan was going to be zero help.

"Okay, well, thanks anyway." Kendall started to turn to leave.

"Just go to his house. He won't mind."

Kendall faced Evan again. She shouldn't go to Brice's house without the man in question offering that as a possibility, but she also didn't want to lose her first big client, her first chance to help plan a proposal, especially with the possibility of a newspaper interview in the near future. Sure, she was working with another client on a hot air balloon proposal, but that wouldn't happen until after the interview. She didn't want to turn down Kellen's business. She couldn't afford to.

Still…showing up at Brice's house felt strange. "I couldn't show up there uninvited."

"Sure you could." Evan batted his hand as if to say her hesitation was silly. "If you have to tell him something, that's your only option. That's the only way I get to talk to him unless he strolls in here." He motioned her toward the cash register and then yanked a piece of paper out of the top of his old banged-up printer. "It's not far from town. I'll draw you a map."

Kendall jiggled her phone. "Or I could just use GPS."

"Brice lives back in the woods, down a dirt driveway. I don't trust the GPS to get you there. He's my next-door neighbor, but it's in a can't-walk-the-distance way." He leaned over a sheet of paper and drew a quick map. "I'll give you my number to call if you get lost." He jotted down his number. "And I actually answer my phone."

True to his word, Evan's map was illustrated with great detail, including sketches of unique places she would pass, like the mailbox shaped like a lady rid-ing a surfboard on a huge wave. Kendall climbed into her car and studied the piece of paper. Brice's house looked easy enough to get to; four turns out of town and she'd be on his road. But Evan had warned that Brice's driveway was easy to miss.

She left the downtown portion of Goose Harbor and drove down a road lined with apple trees; the temptingly sweet smell of their summer blossoms whipped into the car. The next street carried her past a horse ranch, quickly after which both sides of the road became flooded with forests of trees. Despite it being later, since it was summer, she still had sunlight working in her favor. Even still, she slowed her car below the speed limit. With trees so thick and so close to the road, it was almost impossible to see into the next curve of the road, and if a deer jumped out, she'd never avoid hitting it. And even if she did, it would mean driving her car into the trees, which wasn't a better option.

On the next curve the trees split for the space of ten feet and then resumed again. She craned her neck. Was *that* Brice's driveway? If so, she'd know shortly. Evan said if she missed Brice's driveway to continue a half mile up the road and she'd find his driveway and she could turn around there. He'd described what it looked like so she'd be certain. Sure enough, Evan's house and driveway came into view. Although, where Brice's had been a dirt trail between the trees, Evan's was poured concrete leading to a decent-sized Craftsman-style house with a wide terrace porch complete with hanging baskets of colorful flowers.

Not wanting to waste time admiring Evan's home, she completed her turn in the wide driveway and headed back toward Brice's home. This time she found the driveway without an issue and her car bumped down the lane toward a shaded cabin built deep into the woods. Brice's home was less than half the size of Evan's and lacked any sort of trimmings, but somehow that suited Brice.

She parked her car next to his, then climbed up the steps and knocked on the door. Brice answered a minute later in worn jeans, bare feet and a flannel with the sleeves rolled to his elbows, looking every bit the wilderness man his home boasted he might be.

"Kendall." His brow lowered, but the grin pulling his cheeks said she was a welcome surprise.

"I'm sorry to appear uninvited at your place like this."

"I don't mind." He swung the door open wider. "Come on in."

"Thank you." She brushed past him on the way into his home, and her eyes locked with his pale green ones before she skirted her line of vision away to assess her surroundings. The cabin looked like an upscale lodge or the vacation rentals that could be found along the Appalachian Trail. It was built to showcase a floor-to-ceiling fireplace wall. A lingering mix of brewed coffee and grilled steak smell hung in the air. All the furniture looked like Evan's custom creations, and a large red-toned rug tied the whole place together. The lower portion of the home had an open floor plan, and there was a loft upstairs that looked like he might use it as his bedroom. It appeared as if that was all there was to the cabin. It wasn't large, but it was ten times better than the trailer homes she'd grown up in and didn't overwhelm her the way a house like Evan's would have.

"I like your house," she breathed.

He hooked his hand around the back of his neck and looked around as if he was assessing his home with fresh eyes. "It's small."

"No television?"

He shook his head. "No computer or air-conditioning either."

"How do you live?" She swatted at his chest, meaning the question as a joke.

"I own twenty acres and back up to an abandoned summer camp that has a lake with the best fishing this side of Michigan. I don't need a television or computer to stay occupied." Brice's Adam's apple bobbed. "I know it's not a lot. No one else would want to live like this. It's not enough…" His shoulders slumped, not by much, but enough that she noticed.

"Brice. Seriously. Look at me." She snapped her fingers, gaining his attention again. "Your house is great. I like it."

He shrugged. "I learned early on in life not to treasure material possessions."

"You'd hate my place, then. I'm like a little hoarding rat that holds on to everything, I'm afraid." She held her arms up by her sides to make little rat arms in an effort to lighten the mood. "I chalk it up to the fact that my mom and I moved around a lot when I was young. She was always forgetting to pay the rent and we'd come home sometimes to find all our belongings cleared out and the trailer locked up."

He stepped closer to her. "I'm sorry that happened to you."

She bit her lip. Wasn't her goal to *lighten* the mood? Yet she felt safe telling Brice something she'd never said to anyone. "I know it sounds stupid, but to a child, finding out that your beloved stuffed animal has been taken as garbage and you'll never see it again is traumatic. And it didn't happen only one time. I wish."

Brice took a final step and entered her personal space. He brought a tentative hand up to her hair and tucked one of the loose curls around his fingers. "My father was—is—a heavy gambler."

"Brice." She hooked her hand on his wrist and squeezed. "If you don't want to tell me…"

He broke the contact between them and turned away. "You live in Goose Harbor. You're going to find out sooner or later. I'd rather you hear my side than what the rest of the locals think." He paced toward the fireplace, running his fingers over the grooves in the wood that made up the back of his couch along the way.

"Because of my father's gambling addiction, every couple months he'd round up everything of value and sell it. It didn't matter if it was something you'd saved up your own money to buy or something special to you." He laid a hand on top of the bare fireplace mantel. "So it was better to live without something to begin with than have it taken away from you down the road." He touched the scar on his cheek. "I'm not afraid of my father taking my belongings any longer, but I've grown comfortable living without stuff now, so I figured it was better to stay that way. Stay satisfied with a little. You never know what will happen in life. What you'll lose."

Kendall's heart squeezed and she fought the urge to rush over to Brice for a hug. Even though he was an adult and the days of his father taking his possessions were in the past, the memories still burned him. Kendall knew that better than anyone. First from her belongings being tossed as a child during all their evictions, but there were more recent memories too. Ones that hurt so much she couldn't voice them yet. Brice's father had stolen his beloved childhood items, which was horrible. But Kendall's mother had stolen her identity, destroying her credit. If it hadn't been for Sesser Atwood's generous loan, there would have been zero chance of her opening a business. To clean her record she would have had to file a report with the police against her mother, and she couldn't do that. Not to the only family she had.

Brice studied Kendall, but her face was an unreadable mask in the dim light coming in through the windows.

Not for the first time, he chided himself for judging her incorrectly when they met. Between the lines it was easy to comprehend that Kendall had lived through a rough childhood. Not unlike himself. Although hopefully she hadn't been kicked, hit and told she was unwanted on a daily basis. Their similar pasts gave them a mutual respect and understanding of each other. Something he had never felt before. He hadn't told Audra anything about his father, and here was Kendall, whom he'd known only two weeks, and he already felt able to trust her.

He braced his hand on the table. What was happening to him?

Maybe he was going soft as he aged. Maybe he was lonely.

He tried to will Kendall to meet his eyes. *Look at me. You don't need to look downcast around me.*

A knock at the door snapped him out of his thoughts. Was it National Drop In on Brice Day? Had he missed the memo?

Kendall wrapped her fingers around her purse strap. "You were expecting someone? I shouldn't have barged in like this. I'm so sorry. I should go."

"One." He held up a finger. "You didn't barge— I asked you to come in." He held up a second finger. "And two, I wasn't expecting anyone, so this knock is a mystery too."

He discovered his little sister on the other side, which turned his gut into a knot. Finding her on his doorstep close to nine when she had summer school the next day meant trouble at his parents' house.

"What's the matter?" He grabbed Laura's arm and dragged her into the house. His pulse punched against his temples, and his jaw ached—responses to phantom childhood memories, his body's built-in reaction to whenever he heard about his father's bad behavior.

But Laura's gaze landed on Kendall. "Brice!" she hissed. "You have a girl in your house. You never have girls over. I didn't even know you talked to them."

Brice shot Laura a look, letting her know she was overdoing it.

Despite her darker complexion, Kendall's cheeks reddened. "On that note, I should be headed out."

Laura waved her hands. "Not on my account."

"No, don't," Brice answered at the same time as his sister. He moved to block Kendall's retreat. "I'm pretty sure you dropped by to talk about more than my cabin."

"More?" Laura waggled her eyebrows. "Maybe I should leave."

Brice closed his eyes for a second and inhaled warm air. Laura was sixteen. He could only expect her to act like sixteen-year-olds. He had to keep reminding himself that. Calmer now, he opened his eyes. "Kendall, this is my sister, Laura. Laura, this is my friend Kendall."

"Only *friend*?" Laura crossed her arms and turned a pout toward Kendall. "Don't you think he's at least a little bit cute? I mean, in a total grumbly-bear-in-winter sort of way?"

Kendall snickered and winked at Laura. "I'll give your brother more than cute. Between you and me." She latched on to Laura's arm—coconspirators. "I've thought he was the most handsome man in Goose Harbor since the first day I met him," she stage-whispered.

The most handsome? Brice snorted, drawing laughs from both women.

He scrubbed his hand over his jaw. "You do know I'm standing here, right?"

Kendall had to be kidding around for Laura's benefit. No one considered him handsome when he stood beside Evan. His brother had always been his mother's favorite; she'd always said she wished she could have skipped over Brice and had Evan to begin with. *Stop.* Enough of those thoughts for now. He could dwell on them after the women left.

"Wow. Look at that scowl." Kendall pointed his way but was still leaning toward Laura, very quickly becoming his teenage sister's new best friend. "It hadn't crossed my mind before, but you're so right about the grumbly-bear thing."

"All right. Enough foolishness." Brice crossed his arms over his chest and motioned with his head toward the couch. "I've had the pleasure of two ladies showing up unannounced on my doorstep tonight, but neither has told me why yet. Sit down, both of you. Let's get down to business."

Laura and Kendall took the couch and Brice dropped onto the hard ledge near the fireplace.

Laura looked at Kendall. "Go ahead. You were here first."

Kendall smoothed out the flowery skirt she was wearing. "Are you free for a sunset cruise tomorrow?"

"Brice." Laura hissed his name as she bounced to the edge of the couch cushion. "She's asking you on a date!"

Yup, Kendall definitely looked pretty with embarrassment flushing over her cheeks.

"She's not—" Brice started to clarify their relationship for his sister's benefit.

"No." Kendall latched on to Laura's arm. "This is a business proposition. That's all. I have a client who wants to rent the boat for a cruise tomorrow. Are you free to do that?"

A business proposition? Was that really all that was going on between him and Kendall? He studied the way her nose tilted up at the end, her full cheeks and the way her eyes caught the light. She'd been kind and joked with his sister right away, no awkwardness at all. And she hadn't turned and run or looked at him funny after he told her his dad was a gambling addict. That spoke of her character.

Brice rested his elbows on his knees and pressed his palms together.

No. They were not just business partners. They were something more already. A woman didn't share the worst moments of her past with a guy she did business with. At the least, she trusted him, and other than with his family, he hadn't experienced that in a long time. And never with a woman. He'd thought he had with Audra, but he'd been wrong.

Brice grinned. "I'm free. Set it up and call me with times tomorrow."

Kendall's eyes narrowed. "If I call you with times, will you actually answer? Because you didn't today."

"Don't feel bad." Laura tugged out her phone. "He didn't answer my calls either."

Brice felt in his pockets but couldn't locate his phone. "I might have left it at work. What?" His gaze volleyed back and forth between Kendall and his sister, both staring at him as if he'd just said he might have left his brain somewhere. "I don't care about those things. I wouldn't even have one except you insisted." He pointed at his sister.

Laura launched to her feet. "Obviously. We know. But you should care about the people who want to get ahold of you. We're calling you because we need you or we want to hear your opinion on something. That should matter." As she paced she spun on her heels and faced him. "Don't you care about us?"

"I do." Brice held up his hands in surrender. "I care about both of you." He made eye contact with Kendall. "I'll do better. I'm going to try to remember to carry the phone with me for both your sakes." He moved his gaze to his sister. "You tried to call me too?"

"Yeah." She crossed her arms and rocked on her feet. A nervous childhood habit. "Things are weird at home. Can I stay here tonight?"

Weird at home? His pulse kicked up again. "He didn't...didn't hit you, did he?"

Laura rubbed her hand over her forehead. "No, he's

never done that to anyone besides you." Her eyes grew wide and shot toward Kendall. "I'm sorry. I shouldn't have said—"

Brice waved his hand, cutting off her apology. "It's fine." And it was too late now to take it back. "You didn't say anything wrong. I don't care if Kendall knows."

Kendall got to her feet. "It looks like your hands are full here. I should head out."

"Nice meeting you." Laura reached out and squeezed Kendall's hand as she passed.

"You too." Kendall beamed at her. "See you around."

Brice trailed her to the door, flipped on the porch light and followed her outside. Bugs flew in lopsided arcs around the single bulb near the steps. Leaves in the canopy above them whispered like schoolchildren sharing secrets. As they had talked, darkness had crept in. So technically that meant they'd spent the last four sunsets together, and would tomorrow too.

Kendall glanced over her shoulder as he followed her down the stairs. "You don't have to walk me to my car."

"I know I don't have to, but I want to." Why was he following her out anyway? The woods were safe for the most part. It wasn't as if she needed him for protection. Yet he wanted to say goodbye to her—goodnight—without his sister breathing down their necks.

Kendall grinned. "How can a girl argue with that answer?" She hit the button that unlocked the doors to her car and he reached around her, his fingers skimming her waist in order to hold open the door for her. Kendall froze for a heartbeat and then turned around and wrapped him in a hug. It was unexpected, so much so that his hand still held the door handle.

Pressing up onto her toes, she lifted her lips so they

were near his ear and whispered, "You're a good man, Brice Daniels." Then she kissed his cheek. Before he could react she quickly folded herself into the car and shoved it into Reverse.

Brice lifted his fingers to trace over the skin she'd kissed as he turned and watched her brake lights disappear down his driveway.

Chapter Seven

Kendall could do it. She had to.

Pick up the phone and call him.

She'd spent the morning finalizing the details of the hot air balloon date and also exchanged a few last-minute phone calls with Kellen Ashby about the cruise for tonight. Everything was set. All that was left was to call Brice about the time.

She drummed her fingers on her desk.

What had come over her last night? She'd kissed him. Sure, it was a simple peck on the cheek, but it still complicated things between them. A woman shouldn't go around dropping kisses onto the cheeks of every business partner she encountered, and she definitely shouldn't be whispering sweet, encouraging words into their ears either.

She could only imagine what Brice must think of her. Kendall dropped her head into her hands. She'd gone and made the easygoing friendship they'd shared into something messy. After all her steps to prevent that, it had been she who had crossed the line. Brice had always been a perfect gentleman. This was squarely her fault, leading him on like she had. Going forward, she needed to treat him professionally. She'd miss their friendship, but it was the only way to stem the not-so-friendship feelings that swirled around in her chest at the sound of his voice.

Kendall smoothed her hand over her new day planner. It would be better this way. She'd grown too dependent on Brice in the past week and didn't want to be dependent on anyone. Least of all a man. Had a man ever taken care of her? No. She'd taken care of herself, and she would continue to do so.

As she scanned the notes she'd tacked to the wall behind her computer, her eyes landed on the card from Claire and the verse she'd written down.

Isaiah 43:19. *See, I am doing a new thing. Now it springs up; do you not perceive it? I am making a way in the wilderness and streams in the desert.*

Doing a new thing? Hardly. By letting her mind go instantly to a relationship, it looked as if she'd failed at that already. Kendall snatched the verse card off the wall and crumpled it into a ball. Why had she even allowed the verse—a word from God—to bring her any hope? So foolish. God didn't care about her any more than her father had and look how long he'd stayed around. God wasn't doing a new thing in her life—*she* was. She had taken the risks. She had found Sesser and made a deal. If God had cared to take care of her, He would have stopped her mother from ruining her credit. He would have stopped her father from walking away from them.

Life was easier—so much safer—when she acted superficially. Kept everyone at acquaintance level and never knew them deeper and didn't allow them to really know her. When she didn't learn things about people, like that Brice's dad had abused him as a child. Because when she started to get to know people, she started to care, and someday Brice would walk out of her life. Just like her father, just like God and everyone else.

She wasn't someone worth sticking around for. Not worth fighting for.

Being alone by choice was much better than finding out she'd been left alone.

Chatter from customers in the woodworking shop next door filtered through the wall. She hadn't even realized her CD had stopped playing on the computer until now. It had been a sound track of a string orchestra, supposedly meant to soothe a person's stress away. Kendall rolled her shoulders. So much for that.

Kendall tossed the verse card into the waste can and ran her fingers under her eyes, hoping her makeup wasn't a mess from the couple tears that had slipped out. At the same moment the phone rang. She summoned a breath and answered it.

"Love on a Dime."

"Am I speaking with Kendall Mayes?"

"You are."

"Oh, good. This is Jason Moss. I believe Claire told you I'd be calling?"

The reporter.

The bell above her door jingled and she held up a finger, letting whomever it was know she'd be with them in a moment. But her already jarred emotions took a nosedive when her mom plopped down in the chair across from hers. She couldn't deal with her now. Not without risking her chance at an interview, so she put a finger to her lips to let her mother know not to speak.

But Kendall would have to be careful about what she said out loud. When it came to information, everything was ammunition, as far as her mother was concerned.

She summoned her professional persona and silently commanded her voice not to waver. "Yes, Claire mentioned you would be contacting me."

Her mother's eyebrows rose. Kendall shouldn't have mentioned Claire's name.

"Great. I was wondering if you had some time available to sit down with me on Monday. Would eleven work?"

"That would work perfectly." Instead of writing the appointment into her planner where her mother could see it, Kendall jotted it on her palm. She'd transfer the date and time over later when prying eyes weren't nearby. She ended the call with the reporter and took a deep breath as she faced her mother.

Her mother swiveled around in her chair. "Snazzy place you got yourself here, Kenny. I wonder who is paying the bills."

"What does it matter?" Kendall jammed the cap onto her pen.

Mom braced her arm on the edge of the desk. "It matters when you're living like a movie star and your mom is making do spending the night in a homeless shelter."

"What happened to Josh?" When Kendall had left Kentucky, her mother was dating a new man who'd been letting her live with him and was paying for her expenses.

Her mom pulled a cigarette out of her sleeve, but Kendall shook her head.

She tucked the cigarette behind her ear. "Josh found out about Thomas."

"Mom."

"Don't *Mom* me."

Kendall sank her fingers into the armrest of her chair. "Then what about Thomas?"

One of her eyebrows arched. "Unfortunately Thomas isn't going to leave his wife."

Her nails bit even harder into the fabric. "Wait. You were dating a married man?"

"Welcome to the new millennia, Kenny." Her mother lifted her hands and spun in her chair once.

Kendall worked her jaw back and forth. "I don't care what year we're living in. It's still wrong."

"Wrong is relative." She shrugged.

"Actually—"

"For example, what are you doing to get money from that rich tycoon?"

Kendall's heart kicked against her ribs. Her mother couldn't know about Sesser Atwood…could she? There was a chance she was bluffing, waiting for Kendall to slip up and confirm information. Which she wasn't about to do.

Kendall lifted her chin and gathered her paperwork. "I think it's time for you to leave."

"Not until you give me enough money to make it through the weekend. Come on—help your mother out." She held out her hand. "You wouldn't want me to start begging your rich buddy, now, would you?"

If her mother did know about Sesser, then Kendall was doomed either way. Her mother would either blow the secret of their partnership so Sesser would call in his loan and it would ruin Kendall financially, or would stop by for money every week, bleeding Kendall's savings dry under the threat of telling.

Kendall could give her mom money or not. Which was the right path? Neither. But those were the only options she had.

Brice watched the paper lanterns sway along the ceiling of the paddle wheeler as he punched the engine up a notch. Their movement splayed trails of light across the boat's floor, like giant fireflies in the evening air.

Kendall wrung her hands a few feet away from him, looking on as Kellen Ashby stepped up behind Maggie West on the far side of the boat and wrapped his arms around her. Kellen tugged his girlfriend against his chest and nuzzled his chin into her curly hair. The man had agreed to pay a decent sum to rent out the boat for the evening.

Brice positioned the boat far into Lake Michigan right before the sunset. Kendall had turned off the lights, using only the lanterns and some strands she called *twinkle lights* to illuminate the area. Beforehand they'd set up a table with fancy linens and a centerpiece. Kendall had catered in a four-course meal, and she served as waitress for Kellen and Maggie. They ate until the sun dipped below the horizon. She'd hung back, allowing them to enjoy their romantic evening, but she'd also steered clear of Brice.

Because of the kiss? They'd yet to discuss it. And he wouldn't bring it up unless she started hinting about it. Women could be strange that way.

But…no, she was only worried about making certain everything was perfect tonight. For Kellen's proposal, of course, but also because this was her first big planned date for her company. So nerves were understandable. Brice knew he tended to clam up under stress; perhaps Kendall did too. Well, *clam up* usually meant Brice took off into the wilds on his property and camped under the stars until his head cleared, often for days. But thankfully it had been a long time since he needed to do that.

He shifted his weight, gaining the courage to break the silence between them. He would whisper something encouraging, something to coax a smile from her serious expression. Let her know that she was doing a great job and didn't need to be anxious.

Kendall stepped away before he could get a word out and crossed over to the audio controls. She slowly raised the level of music until it was loud enough for everyone on board to hear and enjoy, but not too loud to disturb people in other boats or for the sound to carry over the water.

Brice recognized the voice right away. It was Kellen Ashby singing. Kellen had recently volunteered to function as the worship leader at the newly built church in town because a young pastor had been hired on and had instantly become overwhelmed. Having been the lead singer of a touring band before he became a Christian, Kellen was well suited to be the worship pastor and had the heart to match his talent.

But this didn't sound like one of Kellen's worship songs.

Kendall appeared at Brice's elbow. "It's a love song," she whispered. "He wrote it for her. Isn't it beautiful?"

She used a tissue she held scrunched in her hand to dab at her eyes.

Kellen turned Maggie around in his arms and they started to sway to the music. Maggie's hands crawled up Kellen's back until they found a safe harbor, hooked on his shoulders. Brice started to look away to give them privacy, but his gaze darted back when Maggie screamed.

"Is this…? Am I hearing the words right?" Maggie yelled as she let go of Kellen and started jumping up and down.

Kellen dropped to one knee and pulled a small box from his pocket. Whatever Kellen said was drowned out by the music and the lap of the water against the edge of the boat, but a moment later Maggie launched herself into the man's arms, sending Kellen backward with a hard thud onto the floor. They laughed, neither obviously hurt. Kellen pulled Maggie to her feet, wrapped his arms around her and sealed the moment with a long kiss that neither seemed to want to end.

Kendall whispered, "I think she said yes."

"I'd say so." Brice chuckled.

They stayed out on the water for another hour as the couple held hands, watched stars together and swayed to music. Finally Brice pulled the paddle wheeler back to the shore and helped everyone off at the dock.

Maggie West shook both Kendall's and Brice's hands on the way out. "I want to thank both of you for this wonderful night. I feel like I'm in a dream. I can't believe it. I'm getting married!" She wrapped her arm back around her fiancé.

"No need to thank us." Kendall grinned. "It was all Kellen."

"He's basically wonderful." Maggie rested her hand on Kellen's chest. Even with the darkness cloaking the harbor, the uniquely cut diamond on Maggie's ring glinted.

Kellen curled his fingers over hers. "You both helped to make this a memorable night. Thank you for all you did."

"And you!" Maggie pointed at Kendall. "You rat! You knew about this at Bible study, didn't you? And you didn't say a word."

Kendall held up her hands in an exaggerated shrug. "I guess you'll never know."

"I'll weasel it out of him." She poked Kellen in the ribs. "Thanks to my spies, also known as Kellen's daughters, I know all his ticklish spots."

Their laughter followed them down the dock. Brice stood for a moment, watching them. Maybe he'd been wrong to hold back from dating for so long. He knew Maggie's and Kellen's stories; both of them had faced heartbreak and disappointment in prior relationships. If Brice was being honest, both Kellen and Maggie had borne far worse hurts than the rejected proposal that had made him give up on love. He ran his hand over his jaw. He'd missed out on life, hadn't he? And it was his fault, his only, but he didn't have to continue down that path. His gaze shifted to Kendall.

After Kellen and Maggie left, Kendall stepped back onto the boat and grabbed the step stool from the on-deck closet. She positioned it to start taking down the twinkle lights. Brice followed her back onto the boat.

"Ow!" She snatched her hand away from the ceiling and stuck a finger into her mouth.

Brice steadied her by the elbow. "Are you okay?"

Taking her finger out of her mouth, she shook her hand back and forth as if she was trying to shake away whatever hurt. "Just pinched my finger. I'll live."

"How about you leave those where they are for now? It's late."

"I need them for another event I'm planning." She reached to unhook the strand of lights and almost lost her footing. Why was she balancing on a stepladder in heels anyway?

Brice placed a hand on either side of her waist. The fabric of her dress was soft and warm. "I'll take them down in the morning. I'd rather you not fall or twist your ankle on my boat."

Her head drooped, as if she was praying, and her hands came to rest on top of his. Almost as quickly, she snatched her hands away as if his skin had burned her.

"Kendall," he whispered. "You're not acting like yourself right now. Tell me what's going on in your head. I want to help."

Last night she'd been so open with him, talking about her past and listening to his dark memories. He wanted to rewind and find that Kendall again. Usually silence worked on Brice like a comfortable blanket on a cold night. Usually it soothed him, but tonight silence hurt.

She descended the ladder, but he kept his hands resting on her waistline. "What we did—help make their special moment memorable—that was really great."

"I'm beginning to think we make an excellent team." Brice tried to ease her closer, but Kendall shifted her weight and stepped out of his hold completely.

"Correct. We're a well-matched business team." She nodded but didn't meet his eyes with hers.

He sidestepped and ducked his head to catch her gaze. "Just in business?"

"It's best if that's how it is." She studied the pointy toes of her shoes.

Gently Brice tipped her chin up with two of his fingers. "Best for who?" His whisper died on a groan. She was so close and smelled like flowers and chocolate and he wanted to lean in and discover if her lips would meld to his. "Kendall?" He spoke her name like a question. Asking permission.

She shook her head and turned her back on him. "I think you got the wrong idea last night. I'm not... You're not... It's not like that."

"I see." Brice straightened his spine. "You're sure?"

"Yes. I think... I'm sure."

He shoved his hands into his pockets. "I'm sorry if I made you uncomfortable."

Maybe a camping trip *was* in order. He had a lot to think through. He needed to line up all the reasons why being alone—why not trusting women—made sense so he wouldn't fall into this situation again. This trap. That was what it felt like, and not the safe-release kind. No. Rejection bit through the heart like the metal teeth of a bear trap, severing.

She started to turn back toward him. "Brice, I don't want—"

"Why don't you head home?" He unlatched the entrance door and held it open for her. "I'd rather finish here alone."

She must have sensed that he would have argued with her, or she was simply relieved to leave. That could be it too. Because she didn't fight him as usual. Instead she slipped out onto the pier. She hesitated. "Night and…I'm…I'm sorry."

He couldn't make out her expression in the dark. "There's nothing to be sorry for."

After she left he spent another hour on the boat, taking down the lights and thinking. She'd warned him that she was a serial dater. All but put up red flags, but like an idiot he'd charged ahead. At least she'd stopped him before he made a complete fool of himself, like what he'd done with Audra.

Had anyone ever wanted him? Truly? Audra hadn't.

It's your fault. If you hadn't been born I wouldn't be stuck with your father. His mother's words roared through his mind.

He hopped onto the pier and slammed the paddle wheeler's door shut. Perhaps if he hightailed it home fast enough, he could outrun the voices in his mind. Push them aside.

You're a good man, Brice Daniels.

Yeah? Well, apparently not good enough.

Chapter Eight

Kendall slipped into the second-to-last aisle of church right before the worship song ended. At the front, Kellen Ashby signaled the band to stop playing and everyone's voices joined together to fill the room. Having not grown up attending any sort of church, Kendall didn't know the song, but she wished she did.

She hadn't felt that way in a long time.

Four years ago while she was still in Kentucky, a coworker at the country club she worked at had talked her into attending a women's retreat weekend with her. Little had Kendall known at the time that it was a church-sponsored event. She probably wouldn't have agreed to go if she had known.

Before that weekend, Kendall had acknowledged that God existed. It was all but impossible to see the foothills of the Appalachians every day and not acknowledge that someone had to create them. Beauty like that didn't happen by chance. But acknowledging the presence of a creator and actually submitting to that creator were two very different things.

The retreat weekend with her friend had quickly

chipped away at Kendall's doubts. The women there had been sincere, and they hadn't judged her when she admitted her hesitancy toward trusting in God. That Saturday night Kendall found herself on her knees with her forehead pressed into the ground, crying and asking God to be a part of her life. For the first time ever, she'd fallen asleep believing she was fully loved and accepted. Perhaps if she could have lived at the retreat center with those women forever, she'd still feel that way.

But normal life crashed in on her right away that Monday. Overdue bills and foul words from her mother smacked her back into reality. The feelings of acceptance and love faded and she stuffed the memory of becoming a Christian into the deepest corner of her heart. Sure, she still believed in God and held on to the fact that she was supposed to have an active and growing relationship with Him, but the relationship dissolved quickly into one that looked like an emotionally scarred teenager yelling at and acting out against her foster parents.

That was what God had become to her lately. A foster parent stuck with her, not a father who wanted to adopt her forever. A visitor she should smile for and act politely toward, as opposed to family she could break down in front of and be real with.

People at her old church told her it was wrong to feel that way. Some claimed it was sinful even, but that was how she felt, and if it was evil to think like that, then mark another failure on the list. Another reason for God to turn His back on her.

The seat next to her creaked, causing Kendall to glance over to see who had joined her. Loose blond curls tumbling around her shoulders, Jenna Crest mouthed *hello* and helped her father get situated. Kendall had met Jenna a couple times at the women's Bible study that they both sporadically attended. All of her interactions with the younger woman made Kendall believe Jenna was very sweet and very devoted to taking care of her sickly father and their apple orchard.

At the front, Kellen closed out the worship portion of the service by making a couple announcements—upcoming church picnic, vacation Bible school needs and rules for the end-of-the-month rummage sale—and then he ended with a prayer. "God, I ask that You open the hearts of the people in attendance. Let their hearts be soft and fertile ground this morning for the word You want them to hear. Bless Pastor Song's message, and thank You for being a God who not only meets us here in the sanctuary but wants to meet us in our everyday life. In the name of Your son, Jesus, we ask all these things. Amen."

Pastor Song took the stage and thanked Kellen for leading such heartfelt worship before he launched into preaching. "This morning we'll continue our study through the Psalms by focusing on Psalms chapter nine."

More than a month ago, when Kendall first arrived in Goose Harbor, she'd questioned the wisdom of the church hiring a pastor as young as Jacob Song. He was twenty-eight at most. Not too removed from seminary and he had only two years under his belt of working as an assistant pastor elsewhere. But one Sunday spent listening to his passionate sermons, and Kendall was sold.

As the pastor read over the passage, a line tugged on Kendall's heart. "*Those who know Your name trust in You, for You, Lord, have never forsaken those who seek You.* This translation uses the word *forsaken*, but some others translate the word to be *abandon*. In the history of earth, God has never abandoned someone who sought Him. Not once. Let that sink in."

Kendall sat up a little straighter. That couldn't be right. God had abandoned her, hadn't He? The second life got hard, He felt far away.

The pastor continued speaking. "If we've felt the sting of abandonment, it did not come from God's side of the relationship. Later in Scripture Jesus proclaims that He is always with us and will continue to be until the end of the world. Has the world ended yet? It has not. Despite what your emotions tell you, Jesus stands beside you in the midst of everything you're experiencing today."

Kendall rubbed the palm of her hand back and forth over her chest. The pastor's words were making her heart ache as seedlings of truth, planted long ago, worked their way through the cracks of her childhood pain.

"Believe me." Pastor Song stepped down from the stage to walk into the aisle. "I understand that very often it doesn't feel like God is with us all the time. We struggle because we can't physically see Jesus beside us or feel Him holding our hands on our roughest days. But that is why He has called us to live in community. So we can be the tangible hands of God, caring for one another and blessing one another."

Kendall watched as the pastor walked closer, feeling as if he were speaking directly to her.

"But relationships are hard, aren't they? We're imperfect beings, and no matter how much we don't want to, we're going to end up hurting each other. When we open ourselves up to the people God has placed in our lives, friends, that's a downright scary thing because you are offering your heart with the understanding that within any human relationship there will be pain at some point. But you must, because without community—without relationships—you are not living the fullness of life God desires for you. The beauty of it all is that within the pain of relationships, we learn grace and forgiveness and love—which are some of the most prized attributes in the Bible."

Kendall swallowed around the tightness in her throat. She didn't hear the rest of the sermon because her heart sang so loudly, demanding a response. She wanted to drop onto her knees and cry out to God as she had done at the retreat long ago.

Guilt clawed at her throat, making her tug at the collar of her shirt. She'd shoved so many people out of her life. Every person God tried to place near her she had rejected before anyone had been able to leave her. When she arrived in Goose Harbor she'd planned to live differently than before, and sure, she'd stopped dating, but beyond that, she was the same old Kendall. Tossing every chance of possible friendship aside and keeping her relationships superficial. She'd attended the women's Bible study to meet people, but she'd immediately turned down invitations from Maggie and Paige to join them for lunch or spend time at their homes.

Kendall's eyes found Brice in the sanctuary. He sat six rows forward, to the left, flanked by his sister and his brother. The tilt of his head and his arm let her know he was taking notes. A longing welled in Kendall's heart. She wanted to be seated beside those broad shoulders. The words she'd whispered to him—*you're a good man, Brice Daniels*—were true, and yet they weren't enough. Brice was the best of men. Patient, kind, compassionate and thoughtful—it sounded as though he'd stood in the gap and protected his siblings from the wrath of their father on more than one occasion. She had no doubt that Brice, and perhaps he alone, could understand the scars on her soul that she hid from everyone.

God had placed Brice in Kendall's life for a reason, hadn't He?

And she'd been placed in his to help him. To be God's hands in Brice's life and offer him the opportunity to show his scars too. Yet she'd failed him. Like a spoiled child throwing a tantrum over a gift, she'd slammed the door on their growing relationship the second she felt vulnerable. In doing so, she hadn't only hurt her spiritual growth, but put a roadblock in Brice's growth too.

I'm so selfish. Uninhibited by the fact that the pastor was beginning the closing prayer, Kendall dropped her face into her hands and started to cry. *Forgive me, Lord. I've been so selfish. I've only thought about me and my own pain and haven't considered You or anyone else You've placed in my life. Help me to trust people. I want to do what Pastor Song said—to be Your hands in other people's lives—but I don't know what that looks like. But I'm willing.*

Kendall stiffened as an arm draped around her shoulders.

Jenna squeezed Kendall to her side. "If you want to talk or pray after service, I'm available."

Be open. Be available.

She had to apologize to Brice but couldn't do it right

this second anyway. Even after Pastor Song dismissed the congregation, Brice filed out with his siblings at his side. She wasn't able to catch his eye. Jenna was here and was offering her friendship, and Kendall wasn't about to pass that up.

Kendall scrubbed at her cheeks and smiled at Jenna. "I'd like that very much."

Brice popped the top off the canister of sea salt and sprinkled it liberally over the venison steaks he'd set out on the counter.

Evan headed back to his own home soon after they returned from church, but his sister had asked to stay for the rest of the day. She usually did anymore. They'd opened all the windows to alleviate the stuffy indoor air. His cabin stayed relatively cool due mostly to the thick canopy of trees surrounding his home, but some days he wished he'd invested in a box air-conditioning unit. For today, however, the large ceiling fan and open windows would have to do. Birdsong carried through the screens, providing music. He and Laura fell into their usual, comfortable routine.

His sister sat on a stool with her elbows propped on the kitchen island and her chin in her hand. "You know salt is bad for you, don't you?"

He dumped some grapeseed oil onto the cast-iron grill. "You can't believe everything you read on the internet."

She slapped the top of his counter. "It's not just the internet. The studies come from, like, the national heart research center or something."

The oil pinged in the pan, sizzling as it began to heat. He gave Laura a *you're killing me* look. "Do you want me to make you lunch or not?" As if to tempt her, the smell of the sizzling venison intensified.

"Bring on the salt." She tossed her hands in the air and laughed. "Although, you're using an awful lot of oil there, big bro."

"Are you going to critique my entire meal?"

She tapped her finger on her chin, goading him. "Probably."

"Just checking." He winked at her.

She unzipped the backpack she'd slung onto the counter before church and pulled out a chemistry book for the summer-school course she was taking and a binder. "I love you."

"Good, because you're going to flip when you see the amount of butter I add to the skillet in a minute." He tweaked her nose. "And I love you too, kid."

"I'm not a kid." She flipped open a folder full of schoolwork, but he didn't miss the suppressed smile that flitted across her lips.

"Love you anyway."

He flipped the steaks on the grill to cook the other side; smoke and popping sounds poured from the skillet, a sure sign that the steaks were getting a good searing and would be juicy. His mouth started to water. This was the life. Steaks. Family. What more could he want?

Then again, he couldn't expect Laura to drop in on him forever—to provide company. She was sixteen, but she was taking summer courses with the intention of graduating early. She'd be an adult in the very near future and wouldn't need to run to her big brother for safety anymore. In the next few years she'd go away to college and might leave forever the way their brother

Andrew had. Then what? Brice would be alone for real. Evan might live nearby and be his closest friend, but Evan had his own life, his own interests, and he didn't consider spending the day in the cabin a good time.

Pastor Song had said that people were made to be in relationships. That Brice wasn't supposed to be spending his life alone. Despite his declaration that he would never trust a woman again after having his heart broken by Audra, Brice didn't want to end up a bachelor forever. For a moment he pictured Kendall seated on the stool beside Laura, helping his sister with her homework and joining in as she teased Brice. The image felt so real and right it made his chest ache.

Laura's voice broke through his thoughts. "You know she likes you, right?"

Spatula in hand, Brice froze. "Who likes me?"

"Kendall."

He swiveled to see his sister. How did she know he'd been thinking about the very woman? A chill worked its way over the back of his neck. "How—"

Laura rolled her eyes. "You just said her name. Out loud. While you were cooking."

"I did?" He dumped a ramekin full of butter into the skillet with the steaks and spooned the butter over them as it melted, sealing in the flavors.

She dipped her head in a dramatic nod. "You did. It was creepy. I even looked over at the door to see if she'd come in. When she wasn't there, I thought maybe you had a Bluetooth on. But you're Mr. Kill Technology, so that ruled out the Bluetooth theory pretty quick."

Grease popped on the skillet, showering his arm with tiny stings. "Sorry."

"For what? Liking a girl? It's not as if that's a crime." She pulled her hair together and piled it all into a huge bun on top of her head and then jammed her pencil through the middle of it. "The real issue here is… What are you going to do about it?"

He slipped the spatula under the steaks, eased them out of the pan and then set them on a plate to rest. "About liking Kendall?" It was pointless denying his feelings to his sister. She'd call his bluff in a heartbeat.

She rolled her eyes. "Yes, brainiac."

"Nothing."

"Well, that's stupid."

"Look, Laura." He leaned against the counter and crossed his arms. "It takes two people to want a relationship for one to happen. Kendall has made it clear that she doesn't want me." That he wasn't enough.

Even as he spoke, the pastor's words from earlier came to mind. *But relationships are hard, aren't they? We're imperfect beings, and no matter how much we don't want to, we're going to end up hurting each other.*

Laura frowned. "But she likes you. I know she does."

"You met her once." Brice pulled two plates from his cupboard and dropped a steak onto each one. He probably should have cooked a vegetable to balance out the meal. Next time.

"Once was all it took." She snagged a plate from him and then pointed her fork in his direction. "Besides, weren't you listening in service today? If you feel like you're supposed to be the hands of Christ in her life, then do it with or without a dating relationship. If God has laid her on your heart and mind, He probably wants you to take action on that."

From the mouths of babes…

Laura was right. The dating relationship he desired might never become a reality, but he could still care about Kendall as his sister in Christ. He could serve her and be a tangible example of God's love to her. She needed that, didn't she? Didn't they all?

And going forward, even under the risk of his own heart getting hurt in the process, he would.

For Your Reading Pleasure...

We'll send you 2 books and 2 gifts
ABSOLUTELY FREE
just for completing our Reader's Survey!

YOUR READER'S SURVEY
"THANK YOU" FREE GIFTS INCLUDE:
- ▶ 2 FREE books
- ▶ 2 lovely surprise gifts

PLEASE FILL IN THE CIRCLES COMPLETELY TO RESPOND

1) What type of fiction books do you enjoy reading? (Check all that apply)
- ○ Suspense/Thrillers
- ○ Action/Adventure
- ○ Modern-day Romances
- ○ Historical Romance
- ○ Humor
- ○ Paranormal Romance

2) What attracted you most to the last fiction book you purchased on impulse?
- ○ The Title
- ○ The Cover
- ○ The Author
- ○ The Story

3) What is usually the greatest influencer when you <u>plan</u> to buy a book?
- ○ Advertising
- ○ Referral
- ○ Book Review

4) How often do you access the internet?
- ○ Daily ○ Weekly ○ Monthly ○ Rarely or never.

5) How many NEW paperback fiction novels have you purchased in the past 3 months?
- ○ 0 - 2
- ○ 3 - 6
- ○ 7 or more

YES! I have completed the Reader's Survey. Please send me the 2 FREE books and 2 FREE gifts (gifts are worth about $10) for which I qualify. I understand that I am under no obligation to purchase any books, as explained on the back of this card.

❏ I prefer the regular-print edition
105 IDL GLDG/305 IDL GLDG

❏ I prefer the larger-print edition
122 IDL GLDG/322 IDL GLDG

FIRST NAME   LAST NAME

ADDRESS

APT.#   CITY

STATE/PROV.   ZIP/POSTAL CODE

READER SERVICE—Here's how it works:

► If offer card is missing write to: Reader Service, P.O. Box 1867, Buffalo, NY 14240-1867 or visit www.ReaderService.com ►

BUSINESS REPLY MAIL
FIRST-CLASS MAIL   PERMIT NO. 717   BUFFALO, NY

POSTAGE WILL BE PAID BY ADDRESSEE

READER SERVICE
PO BOX 1867
BUFFALO NY 14240-9952

NO POSTAGE
NECESSARY
IF MAILED
IN THE
UNITED STATES

Chapter Nine

Kendall adjusted the day planner on her desk as Jason Moss took a seat across from her. Tall and slender, the reporter had moppy, dark brown hair, a leather messenger bag and glasses. Honestly he looked like a Clark Kent stand-in.

If only he was some sort of superhero instead of a reporter, because Kendall could use one right now. Minutes before Jason had entered Love on a Dime, her mother made another appearance, asking for more money. Kendall shouldn't have given her all her cash on hand last time, and probably shouldn't have again this time, but what other choice did she have? If Mom breathed a word about her partnership with Sesser, Kendall would lose her business on top of having to pay back the loan. With interest.

The reporter pulled out a click pen and a slender notebook. "Tell me, how did you get the idea to start a dating service?"

Kendall licked her lips and kept half her attention trained on the shadow of her mother outside the front window. Why wouldn't she leave? She had money now.

Go. But she stayed huddled on one of Evan's hand-carved benches.

"Miss Mayes?" Jason cocked his head.

Kendall pressed her hands into her stomach as if the pressure could make the knots inside go away. "I'm sorry. You asked about how I came to the idea, didn't you?"

He answered with a nod, so she continued. She told him about her background in event planning and the years she'd spent helping coordinate weddings and large parties at the country club back in Kentucky. She shared a few elaborate dates that she'd gone on at one time or another, but left out the part about the string of broken relationships that had come along with those dates. "Love on a Dime plans dates and events, but this is not a dating service. I don't match people up or plan to branch into that type of offering in the near future."

Jason adjusted his glasses. "If you ever do start a dating service, I volunteer to be one of your first victims, er, guinea pigs." He tugged at his collar. "It would be great to get my mother off my back about showing up stag at Thanksgiving this year." He chuckled.

Kendall's gaze shifted back to the window when he said the word *mother*. Hers was still out there and it looked as though she was talking to someone, but the angle of the door blocked who. Kendall needed to wrap up the interview as quickly as she could while still being polite. She had to see whom her mother was speaking with.

She turned her attention back to Jason. "Take comfort in the fact that your mother cares so much about you that she wants to see you happily settled."

A grin crept across his face. "In the newspaper world

that's what we call putting a spin on a story. Nicely done, Miss Mayes." He crossed his legs and flipped to a new page in his notebook. "What drives you in this line of business?"

She filtered through the canned responses she and Claire had worked through over dinner on Sunday and then took a deep breath. "It's a joy to help people make memories, and I think that's what this comes down to. Just this past week we had a man contact us to help plan a date so he could propose to his girlfriend. You should have seen her face! That's why I do what I do. I want to hand someone one moment in time where everything is perfect, a moment that they can treasure forever. I believe everyone deserves that." In reality, though, she'd never experienced a moment like that— a span of time when everything was perfect. During every relationship, her father's abandonment had followed her on dates like a third wheel, whispering the whole time that the new guy would leave her too.

Not good enough. Not...enough.

"So you help people get to happily-ever-after?" Jason grinned and jotted something into his notebook.

"You could say that."

"Well, that's great." Jason pinned her with a questioning stare. "But what about you, Miss Mayes? What about your happy ending?"

"I don't follow your question."

"Does the inspiration of Love on a Dime spring from a happily-ever-after in your own life?"

"This isn't about me... This is about the business."

"I know, but is this a situation where those who can't play baseball coach instead?"

Who was her mother speaking with outside? "That's not how that phrase goes."

"You haven't answered my question."

Kendall took a large breath and tried to remember how Claire had told her to answer questions. "My happily-ever-after *is* this business. It comes from helping others. That's what I care about."

"But the dates aren't inspired by your own romantic life?"

"I'm afraid that some of us don't get the happy ending we dreamed of, which, of course, is why the special moments in life are even more important." She forced a smile.

"Describe for me a few examples of dates you might plan."

Kendall launched into the details of the hot air balloon date and a scavenger hunt date and then made sure to mention about the weekly sunset cruises. Just as they were wrapping up the interview, the bell above her door jingled and Claire Atwood stepped inside.

She jogged over to the desk and squeezed Jason's arm. "I've been calling and texting you like crazy."

Jason pulled his phone out of his bag. "I always turn it to Silent during an interview. You know that."

"I wish I'd recalled that sooner. I looked all over town for you before I remembered you'd be here. I have the best news. It's the very best news I've ever received."

Even with the threat of her mother hovering outside the door, it was impossible not to start smiling at Claire's obvious excitement.

"Tell us, then." Jason laughed.

"The adoption went through." Her voice rose an octave. "I finally get to bring Alexei home." She bounced on the balls of her feet.

Jason launched out of his seat. "You're right. That *is* the best news I've heard all day." He leaned in for a hug. "You have a son! You're a mom!"

"Congratulations." Kendall stood up. "That's so exciting. When will Alexei be here?"

Claire pulled a photo out of her purse. "It's an international adoption. He lives in Russia, so I'll have to fly there and then stay through court proceedings." She handed over the picture. A little boy with large, soulful brown eyes stared out through the image. "He's six."

"He's adorable." Kendall handed the picture to Jason.

Jason studied the little boy. "I'm so proud of you, coz."

"Coz?" Kendall tilted her head, considering Claire and Jason. "As in cousin?"

"Yeah." Jason slung his arm around Claire's shoulders. Now that Kendall compared them, they did have the same-shaped nose and shared height. "Our moms are sisters."

Which would make Jason Sesser Atwood's nephew. Local reporter must be a great person for the wealthy tycoon to be related to. No wonder Jason had promised to do a front-page spread about her business. Her success was Sesser's success. Not that the man didn't have the right to use every avenue to help promote his businesses, and she appreciated it too, but she wished Claire and Sesser would have been up front about the connection. Kendall would have been more relaxed for the interview if she had known Jason would write a positive article no matter what she said.

The bell over the door rang again, drawing Kendall's gaze. Brice stood on the threshold with a bouquet of pink gerbera daisies in hand.

Claire glanced over her shoulder, and her expression fell. "Looks like it's time to leave, Jay." She looped her arm through her cousin's. Jason gave Kendall a salute and told her the article would run in the next paper, end of the week. He also mentioned to her that he planned on submitting his article to bigger publications and that sometimes they were picked up for wider circulation. After Claire and Jason exchanged awkward hellos with Brice, they headed out into the downtown portion of Goose Harbor.

"Brice." Kendall breathed his name. There were so many things she wanted to say. "Sorry" ranked high on the list. Yet somehow words failed at the moment. She'd rather stare at his broad shoulders and his strong jaw and enjoy the fact that he'd sought her out. That wasn't normal practice for the men she'd met in her life. No one ever fought to keep her. Not to say that was what Brice was doing. But he was here—with flowers. That had to mean something.

Brice worked his jaw back and forth. "I saw your mother down the sidewalk. Was she in here bothering you?"

Kendall cupped her hand over her forehead. "Yes. Today, and yesterday, and the day before."

His boots ate up the distance between the door and her desk. "You've got to put a stop to it."

"How? What can I possibly do?"

"File a police report."

"On my mother? I couldn't. Isn't that going against

what God wants? There's that whole 'honor thy mother and father' part of the Ten Commandments."

Brice shook his head. "Honoring doesn't mean allowing yourself to be manipulated. You're an adult now. You don't live under her roof any longer. And she's an adult who needs to accept responsibility for her problems." He looked down at the flowers in his hands. "If it makes you feel better, I had to file a report against my father a few years back to get him to stop showing up at my house."

"You did?"

"I did. And God hasn't sent a lightning bolt to smite me just yet." He winked.

"But she's threatened to say things about me... What will everyone think?"

He stepped around the desk to stand right in front of her and then pressed the bouquet into her hands. "Those of us who know you and care about you will always believe the best about you." He kept his hands on top of hers as they both cradled the flowers. "We also know that, no matter what she says, you're not the person you might have been yesterday. We're new every morning, complete with fresh starts."

The warmth of his hands on top of hers and his softly spoken words made Kendall's pulse zing through her veins. "These are beautiful."

His gaze shifted to something more intense. "You're beautiful."

Kendall swallowed hard. "I'm going to put these in water." She slipped her hands away from his, laid the bouquet on her desk and then opened her drawer to find her scissors. When she located them, her hands slipped, she fumbled the shears and the point cut across her palm. A flash of white-hot pain radiated from the cut. She fisted her hand. "Ow!"

Brice grabbed her elbow. "What happened?"

"I cut my hand." Blood seeped out of the side of her fist. She shouldn't have been moving so fast while she was flustered. But why was Brice here? The last time they'd spoken, really spoken, was days ago when she'd told him she only wanted a business relationship. After that they'd exchanged a tense Friday night sunset cruise and then hadn't spoken all weekend. She'd assumed their friendship would end after that, especially after he had ignored her at church. "Grab me a paper towel?"

"Is it deep? You might need to go to the hospital."

She flexed her hand, examining the cut. It was gross, but not deep enough to require stitches. "I'm fine. I'll be good after the blood stops."

"Kend—"

"I'll even go to the police department and file a report."

"You will?" He sounded surprised.

He was right. She needed to deal with her mother or else she'd never be free to start fresh here. And she badly wanted that, more now than ever before. Her eyes skirted to his. "I will."

He handed her a paper towel but still looked as though he was ready to launch into protector mode. "I'll drive you there right now."

Brice paced the interview room in the police department like a caged circus lion, growing angrier and angrier as Kendall detailed her story for Officer

Wright. The radio attached to a loop on the officer's uniform bellowed static intermittently.

The officer nodded, encouraging Kendall to continue. "So your mother stole your identity?"

"Yes. But you aren't going to arrest her, are you? I don't want her arrested." Kendall shot a frightened look Brice's way. "If you're going to do that, then I want to stop the report."

Officer Wright laid down his pen. "The identity theft didn't occur in our jurisdiction. Since it sounds like the illegal actions took place in Kentucky, a case would have to be filed against her there. What we're doing here today is learning how to keep you safe in Goose Harbor. I need the background details in order to write a report." He spoke in a calm and even voice, more than likely a product of his training. "Once you have the report, we can look at getting a court order that says she's not allowed to contact you. That's what we're working toward right now."

Should Brice feel relieved that her mother wouldn't get arrested? At the moment, he wasn't. He wanted immediate and total justice for Kendall. Just like he wished his childhood self, crouching and trembling in the closet, could have been given justice. Dad had been arrested many times, but never for what he'd done to his family.

Kendall took a deep breath. "Okay. Then yes. You know those credit card offers that come in the mail? The ones that say you've been selected for an amazing deal? Without my knowledge she filled out a bunch of those in my name and then maxed them all out. She destroyed my credit. I never filed a report on her, though, because she's all the family I have and I didn't want her to be arrested."

"So she compromised your Social Security number?"

Kendall nodded.

Brice turned and paced the room again, fisting and unfisting his hands. A gladiator of purpose took shape within his mind. Going forward, he'd protect Kendall any way that he could. With a deadbeat dad and a completely selfish mother, Kendall had been betrayed by the people who should have been there to comfort and take care of her during her formative years. No wonder she'd turned to serial dating. She was probably looking for someone—anyone—to tell her she was worth loving. And she'd mentioned before that she was always the one to break up first, which made sense with her background. Hurt before she got hurt. College students learned that in Psychology 101.

Kendall traced a finger on her good hand across the edge of the table in the room. "Since she showed up in Goose Harbor, she's been asking for money. Each time she's threatened to ruin me here if I don't give her more."

The officer pursed his lips. "And have you been giving her more money?"

She adjusted the paper towel in her cut hand. More blood had seeped through. She hadn't even properly cleaned the injury before coming to the police station.

"I have." Kendall confirmed Brice's suspicion.

He hadn't realized his growl was audible until both Kendall and the officer stopped talking and turned to stare at him.

"Brice, maybe you should wait out in the hall. I can do this," Kendall assured him.

"No. I'll behave. I want to stay with you." He moved next to the officer and eased a first-aid kit down from a hook on the wall. "I just don't like to hear about you being treated like that. You should have been taken care of." He took the empty seat next to Kendall and reached for her injured hand, turning it palm up, her slender fingers resting along his wrist. "You deserve to be taken care of." She winced as he cleaned out the cut with rubbing alcohol but allowed him to keep cradling her hand.

Officer Wright cleared his throat. "Starting today, stop giving her money. I don't care what she says or threatens, don't do it. If she shows up and you feel uncomfortable, call us right away. That's what we're here for."

Brice lifted her palm close to his lips, blowing on it lightly to dry the area. Dabbing the cut with ointment, he finished the process by wrapping her hand in gauze. Once done, he draped his hands around hers and held it on his lap. She looked down at their hands for a moment, then met Brice's gaze and smiled.

They left the police station with a report number in hand and instructions to call the department in a few days for a copy of the write-up. It wouldn't fix the problem with her mother, but it was a step in the right direction. A step he'd been able to help her take. His heart swelled.

Brice held open the passenger door to his car. "Can I take you for ice cream?"

Kendall moved to sit down but then spun around and grabbed his wrist. "I need to tell you. I'm sorry for how I treated you. On the boat. It was wrong. I was scared. And—"

"It's okay." He rested his hand on the vehicle's roof, above her head. "I'm sorry too."

Her brow scrunched. "But you were—"

"Grumpy? Terse? Rude?"

She tapped his chest. "I think *terse* and *rude* by definition are the same thing actually."

He couldn't hold back his goofy grin. Kendall was a match for him. She lightened up his too-serious moments and forced him to remember that there were things worth celebrating every single day. "All right, Miss Thesaurus, you haven't answered my question. Can I take you out for ice cream?"

She squeezed his wrist before letting go. "I'd like that a lot."

He drove her past the downtown portion of Goose Harbor and finally parked near the beach. "There's a small shop that sells hand-churned ice cream. It's the best-kept secret in town."

At Klingman's Creamery she ordered a waffle cone with chocolate marshmallow ice cream, and he went old school and got the sugar cone with vanilla dipped in sprinkles.

"I'm not a big chocolate fan," he explained as they strolled out toward the beach. Their shoulders bumped as they walked close together.

"Pity." She pouted. "But I guess it's a good thing in the end. There's more chocolate available in the world now for me." They took a few steps before she let out a long breath. "Did I do the right thing? Reporting my mother?"

"You did."

"It feels wrong. I feel guilty. Aren't we supposed to turn the other cheek?"

Tough question, but thankfully it was something he'd struggled with for most of his adult life, so he could give her a gut-level answer. "Turning the other cheek doesn't mean allowing yourself to get walked on. It's not honoring God to let people use you or to accommodate any sinful behaviors they might have."

"I guess that makes sense."

He pointed to an empty bench along the boardwalk and they both sat down and stared out into the lake. The silence between them was comfortable. This was what Brice had envisioned all those years ago when he considered the idea of growing old with someone. Why had he ever thought Audra, who filled every lull with chatter and wanted to go out every evening and never took time to breathe, was a good match for him?

Kendall finished her cone long before he did. "Brice? Can I ask you a serious question?"

"Sure."

"A guy like you... There are a lot of available women in this town—really great women."

Knowing what she was getting at, he stalled for time. "I don't think that's a question."

"Why are you single?"

Be honest. Open up. "No girl in her right mind ever wanted me."

"I don't believe you're that insecure." Her fingers grazed his arm. "Wait. Are you? *Brice*," she hissed. "That's ridiculous. How could you think that? You can't say they don't want you unless you've asked. And I haven't seen you going around asking girls to marry you, so—"

"I did ask and she said no."

Kendall's face fell. "Oh."

"You know my cabin? I bought that place with money I'd been saving all through college. I had a girlfriend at the time. Her name was Audra Byrd. I thought I was in love." He shrugged. It felt strange even saying "love" and "Audra" in the same sentence. What they'd had was never love. Not even close.

"I know now it was more physical attraction than anything. She was beautiful and I was a man." He looked at Kendall for the first time. *You're beautiful too, but it's so much more than your appearance.* "We would have been miserable together. She wasn't a Christian. There's no excuse. I was stupid. She was adventurous and she pressured me to go further and further. I thought I had finally found someone who wanted me. Someone who valued me for who I was."

His mother's voice pitched through his mind. *You were never wanted. My life would have been better if I hadn't gotten pregnant with you.*

"You don't need to tell me this stuff." Kendall laid her hand on his knee.

He tossed the rest of his ice-cream cone in the nearby garbage can. "I want you to know." He shifted on the bench so his hand sat beside hers. "I asked Audra to marry me and she laughed in my face. I wasn't good enough for her. I was a joke. She'd been using me the whole time because I paid for everything and bought her whatever she asked for. Money had become a form of love for me... We can thank my father for that." After that he'd returned to Goose Harbor to live in the cabin alone, where he'd rid himself of needless possessions. He determined that if someone ever did come into his life again, he needed to know that money wasn't part of the equation in their relationship.

"I'm so sorry."

Might as well tell it all. "I found out later she was seeing another guy too. It cut me up for a long time. I wasn't good enough for her. The life I had to offer a woman—it's not good enough." He focused on the sand at his feet. Anything to not look at Kendall as he spoke. "I don't ever want someone to regret being with me. To feel stuck."

Like his mother had been. Stuck in her horrible life with her abusive husband, all because Brice had the audacity to be born.

Kendall moved her hand on top of his and offered a squeeze. "Not every girl is Audra. I'm sorry she hurt you so much."

He slipped his hand out from under hers and raked it through his hair. "It's not that big of a deal."

"It is if it's holding you back." She spoke softly.

"It's not holding me back. I don't feel—"

"I get that you're scared, but you're allowing something that happened a long time ago to drown you. You're stuck until you forgive her, and I think deep down you know that."

They took the long way back to his car and didn't speak much on the drive to drop her back at her office, where she'd left her car. Brice was too lost in thought.

Forgive Audra? He clamped his teeth together. What a foolish idea. Audra held no power over him any longer. He was fine. He'd moved on. He had proven that he was better off without her the same as he'd long ago done where his father was concerned.

Chapter Ten

Kendall pushed the hold button on the third call and answered the incoming one. "Love on a Dime. Can I take your number and call you back?"

"May I speak to Kendall Mayes?"

Kendall wrapped her hand around her lukewarm coffee mug. She'd planned on starting the day slowly with some time spent drinking the caramel latte she'd made a special stop for at the cute, local shop, Fair Tradewinds Coffee. She counted the treat as her reward for all her hard work over the past month, but it looked as though a relaxing morning wasn't going to happen.

"Speaking." She bit her lip and watched the blinking lights signaling the other waiting callers. The first one was a radio station from the nearby large city of Brookside wanting to schedule an on-air interview to showcase her company. The second was Joel Palermo, a Goose Harbor firefighter trying to schedule a sunset cruise date as a surprise for his girlfriend. The third was an energetic couple from Ohio who wanted her to plan an entire weekend for them full of what they called "romantic dune camping." Kendall wasn't sure how romantic camping on the dunes could be, but she'd research it and plan them the perfect getaway anyway.

Ever since Jason's article about Love on a Dime had run in the paper and had been featured on a few travel websites, business had been steady. More than steady. It was beginning to take over all her time. So much so that Kendall was considering the possibility of hiring an assistant soon. Who knew one little article could create such a stir? Then again, Jason had warned her that he'd be submitting his work for larger publications to pick up. She should have taken him seriously. Or maybe Sesser had other favors to call in with newspapers and that was why she was getting so much publicity. Whatever the reason, Kendall was thankful.

"My name is Sandy. I'm one of the feature writers for *Midwestern Traveler*. Have you heard of us?"

Kendall choked on her sip of coffee and started to cough. "I'm sorry." She caught her breath. "The award-winning travel magazine? You're only my favorite resource for travel planning! Of course I've heard of you." *Midwestern Traveler* had been the publication that started her love for Goose Harbor. They'd featured Ring Beach, Goose Harbor's pristine oval-shaped swim area complete with powdery beaches and calm waves, in their top five places to visit in the entire Midwest, and the next article followed up with a feature dedicated to the tourist town. Those two articles had made Kendall's decision about where to start her business easy. Goose Harbor had been highlighted as a friendly place filled with beauty. It had lived up to all her dreams.

"We'd like to run a feature on your company."

"A whole feature article? On me?"

"Yes. I'd planned an outing to Goose Harbor for this weekend before I heard about your business, and now it seems like perfect timing. Would you be able to meet me for an interview?"

"Yes. Of course. Name the time." Kendall scribbled down the time and location as she ended the call and switched over to the first one on hold. She and Sandy would meet at Fair Tradewinds Coffee on Friday morning, and Sandy said she was planning to write the article that same day in order to send it on to her editor so it could be squeezed in for the next publication.

It was long past noon when the bells over Kendall's front door jingled, letting her know someone was entering her side of the divided storefront. Brice's sister offered a hesitant wave as she walked toward her desk.

"Laura." Kendall pushed her pile of paperwork to the side of her desk and smiled. "It's so nice to see you, but is everything all right?" As much as the sight of Brice's little sister made Kendall happy, she had to wonder why she was here. Was Brice hurt? He wasn't good about using his cell phone. Perhaps he'd sent Laura to relay a message for him. Kendall's heart sped into a double-time march. "Is Brice okay?"

"Don't know." Laura shrugged. "Haven't seen him." She plopped into the empty seat on the other side of the desk. "Haven't talked to him today either."

"Oh." Kendall forced herself to take a few longer breaths. Maybe Laura had stopped by to find her other brother, but Evan wasn't in his woodshop? He tended to close up around lunchtime to eat at one of the diners in town. "And Evan...?"

"He's in his shop." Laura bit her bottom lip. "I came to see you."

"I'm glad you did. I didn't mean to make it sound like you weren't welcome. I hope you know that." Kendall backpedaled. She'd never been great at having friendships with other women, let alone speaking to them. Hopefully she hadn't sounded rude. "How can I help you?"

"I want your advice." Laura let out a puff of air that stirred her long bangs.

Kendall swallowed hard. She didn't consider herself the best role model for a teenage girl. She'd made one too many mistakes in her life to be able to offer sound counsel to anyone. "You want advice? From me? Laura, I'm—"

"Of course from you. You're basically my brother's girlfriend, so I know you know a thing or two about relationships."

Brice's girlfriend? She gulped. She couldn't let Laura have the wrong impression. She and Brice were friends—good friends—but that was all. "We aren't dating. Seriously, it's only business."

Laura leaned her head so she was looking up at the ceiling and spun the wheeled chair in a circle. "You two are so dating. Don't even deny it." She put her feet on the ground, stopping the spinning as she faced Kendall again. "You're all Brice talks about anymore."

"I am?" She fumbled the pen she'd been holding and it bounced off the desk, falling with a clank to the floor.

Laura grinned and picked up the pen. "Does that surprise you?"

"I just…" Kendall shook her head. "What did you

want to talk about?" She pressed her hand against her stomach as it grumbled. She really shouldn't have skipped lunch.

"So, there's this guy in the youth group that I really like."

Ah. Okay. Boy problems. "Go on."

"He's cute. I'm talking tall, star-of-the-basketball-team cute." Laura played with the pen, making it weave through her fingers. "You know what I mean, right?"

Kendall winked at her, trying to calm the girl's nerves. "I think I know the type."

"I can't talk to my brothers about this because… well, they're my brothers and they want to pound any guy who looks at me."

"I could imagine they would." She pictured a teenage boy cowering between the strong pair that made up Brice and Evan and had to bite back a laugh. With Brice's muscular build and Evan's quick wit, a poor guy wanting a date with Laura wouldn't stand a chance. Kendall pushed back against the hurt she felt every time she was reminded that she'd never had a man in her life—no father or brother—who wanted to protect her like that. Though she no doubt found it annoying now, Laura didn't know how blessed she was to have them.

Laura's eyebrows dove. "You won't tell Brice, will you?"

Kendall didn't want to make a promise to withhold information from Brice, so she hedged with "What would there be to tell?"

Laura leaned forward in her chair. "His name is Drew Foster. That's a good name, right? He goes to the private high school in Shadowbend, but his family comes to our church." She lowered her voice. "He and I have been sneaking out of youth group when everyone breaks into their small groups and we've been going for walks out behind the church. There's a trail that leads down to the beach."

Alarms sounded in Kendall's mind. She wanted to hunt down Drew Foster already and give him a piece of her mind for dragging Laura out of church, but Kendall bit her tongue and nodded, encouraging Laura to share more. Shutting down the girl now would only lead to her hiding information, and if Kendall was going to be of any help, she needed to know everything.

"A few weeks ago it went from going on walks to us rushing down to the beach to make out."

No, no, no. "Oh."

Laura stabbed the pen through the bun on top of her head and frowned. "But he says we can't be boyfriend and girlfriend, at least not in public. Supposedly his parents aren't cool with him dating in high school, so we have to keep it a secret, and our friends at youth group can't know because he has a reputation to keep up. What does that even mean?"

Kendall's mouth opened and then closed and then opened again. Which one of the multiple issues should she begin addressing? How could she speak the truth in love without scaring Laura away? She wanted to be a safe place for Laura to share, especially if the girl had no women to talk with about these situations, but she also couldn't encourage the behavior Laura had shared with her.

Please help me say the right words. To say what

*she needs to hear. Let me be Your hands and feet for
Laura.*

Kendall traced her fingers over her day planner.
She needed to tell Laura what she wished someone
had told her so many years ago. "It means that you
should steer clear—very, very clear—of Drew Foster."

"But—"

Kendall held up her hand. "Believe me, Laura, I
hate to admit it, but I've been down that road with a
guy or two and it never leads to anywhere good. Take
it from a girl who's had her heart broken one too many
times. A guy who won't acknowledge his tie to you in
public is not worth any piece of you. Not your attention and definitely not your affection."

"I think…" Laura stared down at the floor. "I think
he loves me, though."

Yes, Kendall wanted to find Drew Foster and give
him a huge talking-to. "Has he told you that he does?"

"No, but he wouldn't want to make out with me so
much if he didn't."

Kendall sucked in a shaky breath. "Some men—not
all, but some of them—actually will. God says we're
supposed to guard our hearts, and that means that we
have to be careful about the type of guys we hand our
hearts to." Guilt surfaced in Kendall's heart. She had
no right to say this to Laura, not when Kendall had
done a terrible job guarding her heart. But she pressed
on anyway, saying the words she wished someone
would have cared enough to say to her as a teen. "Do
you think a guy who pulls you away from your small
group at church and asks you to lie to everyone and

only spends time with you doing physical things is the type of guy God wants you to spend time with?"

"But he's the only guy who likes me."

"That's probably not true. A lot of the good guys are shier and quieter about liking someone. It takes time to find the really great ones, but I promise you, the great ones are never the guys who take you away from something like church time."

A sly smile crept its way across Laura's face. "The quiet ones like my brother, huh?"

"He's a good one," Kendall acknowledged. Brice was the best man she'd ever met.

"He is. Don't break his heart."

"We're not…" Kendall leaned back in her chair. Laura would badger her until she gave in, so she added, "I don't plan on hurting him."

Laura nodded. "It's kind of nice, talking to another woman about this stuff. My mom's not…not the type you want to share with."

"Mine either." Kendall picked up her now-cold coffee cup and worked it around and around in her hands. "You need to know that you have so much worth, Laura. You're a smart and determined young woman. Don't settle for being treated poorly. Don't settle for anyone who isn't proud to walk through the center of town with his arm around your shoulders, okay?"

"Okay."

"And don't make out with a guy until you're in a committed relationship. Or married. How about married? Just stick with that." Kendall winked.

Laura rolled her eyes. "Now you're sounding like an old person."

"That's because I *am* an old person."

* * *

Brice slipped his hands into his pockets as he exited Goose Harbor Bank and Trust. With a wave, he passed Caleb Beck and his obviously pregnant wife, Paige, on the sidewalk as they were leaving the Cherry Top Café.

In the past, Brice had avoided the downtown portion of Goose Harbor at all costs. Fighting through the tourist crowds and being stopped by other locals for chitchat hadn't appealed to him. Lately, though, he hadn't minded it so much. He'd never be an extrovert, it simply wasn't his personality, but he'd discovered he could be around people, even large groups, for a short time span and enjoy the experience. Apparently Kendall was rubbing off on him.

In fact, a lot of pieces in his life had changed so far this summer. A month and a half ago he was discussing the possibility of having to sell off some of his boats and perhaps rework his company altogether in order to survive. Now he was socking away money into a new savings account each week, and his dream of fighting Sesser and building a second working pier in town finally didn't look so far out of grasp. Sure, it wouldn't be possible for another year or more, but still, he had hope now, and hope was powerful.

Members of the Goose Harbor Chamber of Commerce were busy setting up a music stage and booths in the square for the three-day Venetian Festival that took place midsummer every year. The streets were already roped off and open to pedestrians only, and the event didn't even start until nightfall. The carnival atmosphere culminated on the third evening with a boat show just off famous Ring Beach and a fireworks display.

Brice veered down the sidewalk toward the building that Kendall and Evan shared. As much as he was warming up to being out and about more, Brice wasn't ready for the crush of people the Venetian Festival would draw. He hadn't signed any of his boats up for the event, even though he probably should have to advertise the sunset cruises.

He pushed through the front door of Love on a Dime and then froze. His sister and Kendall sat together around Kendall's desk, sharing a bag of microwave popcorn. "Laura? What are you doing here?"

His sister tossed a piece of popcorn at his chest. "Hanging out with this woman, who, might I add, is far too good for the likes of you, Grumbly Bear."

Brice's eyes met Kendall's, and his heart kicked against his ribs at the sight of her wide smile. "You're right—she is far too good for me."

"You guys! I'm standing right here." Kendall got to her feet and crossed her arms over her chest in mock offense.

"Seriously, though." Brice winked at her and stepped closer. "What were you guys talking about?"

"Oh." Kendall grinned at Laura in a conspiratorial way. "Just girl stuff."

Brice grimaced, making them both laugh. They could have their girl talks without him. "I don't want to break up your fun, but I have some news to share."

Laura patted the chair next to hers. "So spill."

Brice stayed standing near Kendall. "I got word today. We're finally set to move our boat to the pier in town and start running our sunset cruises from there."

Kendall clapped her hands, screamed in a high-pitched way and then launched herself into his arms for a hug. "Thank you. Thank you. Thank you."

It had taken days of wrangling prices back and forth with Sesser's daughter, Claire, before he'd signed a yearlong contract to dock his boat there, but all the hassle was worth Kendall's reaction.

The front door flew open and Evan jogged into the shop, still wearing his heavy tool belt. He stopped a few feet from them as his gaze bounced from Kendall to Brice to Laura. He shook his head, smiling. "Here I think I'm running to the rescue. I heard a scream and figured poor Kendall is next door all alone and some spider or mole got into her place and she needs help." Evan sauntered closer. "Instead I find my entire family hanging out with her when I'm only twenty feet on the other side of that wall." He laughed. "Shows how I rate."

"Aw." Laura jumped up and gave him a hug. "You know we love you."

"You'll have to tell me your secret, Kendall." Evan draped his arm over their sister's shoulders and pulled her tight against his side.

Obviously not realizing Evan was joking, Kendall worked her bottom lip between her teeth. "We didn't plan to exclude you. I didn't know they were stopping by or—"

Brice slung his arm around Kendall's waist. "Sorry, Ev. She's prettier than you, man."

Kendall, Laura and Evan spent the next twenty minutes teasing each other and talking about their plans for the Venetian Festival. Brice hung back out of the conversation in order to soak the moment in. He couldn't remember a time in the recent past when his siblings had been so happy together. Not just his siblings, but him too. The burden on his shoulders felt lighter today. With a sigh, he pulled Kendall a little closer to his side and thanked God for the changes in his life.

Chapter Eleven

For his mother to call him, she must have been desperate.

Brice put his car in Park and unbuckled his seat belt, but stayed in the vehicle. Paint peeled off the sides of his parents' home and the roof sagged; it looked as though it was leaking through in four or five places. Water was probably causing major structural damage. Creeping Charlie along with a host of other weeds had taken over the front yard.

The worst decision he and Evan ever made was to help his parents finally purchase their childhood home from Sesser Atwood. It burned Brice to admit it, but his mom and dad had been better off continuing to rent the property from Atwood. At least then repairs came out of the tycoon's pocket. When they were still renting, Sesser was constantly threatening to have them thrown out. Then again, the man had a right to, since Brice's dad was always months behind on paying. Brice sighed. Sometimes it was difficult to know what the right or best choice was, even in retrospect.

He pinched the bridge of his nose for a moment before finally shoving out of the car. He grabbed his tool-box from the truck and then made his way around the cracked asphalt to their front door. The four wooden steps up to their porch groaned under his weight. Rotted.

His mother opened the door for him, a scowl causing her to appear more wrinkled than she was. "I wasn't going to call you." She trailed after him as he picked his way through the front room and made a beeline toward their laundry room.

In the past ten years his mother had slowly become what could only be classified as a hoarder. Some rooms contained only a narrow walking path, while in others he had to crunch over clothing and trash to pass through. A ball of frustration formed in his gut. His sister shouldn't have to live like this. He needed to talk to Laura. Convince her to move in with him for the rest of her high school career and then help her fill out applications for financial aid for colleges. She had to leave town, get away from their parents. He wouldn't let them hold her back.

His mother kept following him. "But your father's been MIA for the past few weeks and Evan didn't return my call, so all that was left was you." Translation: *I didn't want to call you. You were my last choice. Like always.*

Brice ground his molars together so hard a pain shot into his temples. "Can you tell me what's been happening with the washer again?"

She detailed the sounds the washing machine had been making and showed him where water pooled on the floor behind it. He'd fixed the same washer twice already. It was long past life support.

Brice rubbed his palm back and forth against his jawline. "With all the problems this one has given you, I could just buy you a new one. One that wouldn't—"

"We're not starting on that. Not again." She folded her arms. "If you came here to tell me my belongings don't meet your standards, then you can just go right on back home."

Tightness pulled across his chest. "Mom, you know it's not like that."

For a moment their eyes met and she glared at him, hard and cold. *Why?* Why did she insist on believing the worst about him? Why couldn't she be proud? Why couldn't she love him? Throat burning, he swallowed his words and held her gaze.

She shuffled away without another word, so he went to work taking the machine apart. Brice used the back of his hand to wipe sweat off his forehead. The small, closed room he worked in was heating like a tin can left out in the sunshine. Ants marched in a line by the hundreds along the opposite wall. He tried not to consider what other critters might infest their home. Bugs and vermin didn't bother him when they were out in nature, but pests shouldn't reside in the home his sister lived in.

Thankfully it didn't take long to find the issue. The rubber on the drive belt was worn and cracked in a few places. It needed to be replaced. A quick trip to a big-box hardware store in the next town over solved the problem. When he returned to his parents' home, it took only thirty more minutes to install the new belt and put the machine back together.

His mother waited in the front room as he carried out his toolbox. "It should work just fine for you now."

"Let's see if this fix lasts any longer than your others did." She didn't look up from the year-old magazine she pretended to flip through. Perched on the edge of a ratty chair, she looked fragile. His mother had always been a small woman, but stress and life had worn her down to bones over skin. All sharp points and no padding.

His jaw throbbed from holding in words. He turned to leave but froze. Kendall had faced the troubles she had with her mother, faced them like a trouper. He'd spotted Kendall's mom near the docks a few times, but Kendall said that after telling her mother about the police report, so far, the woman was leaving her alone. Kendall had taken steps to deal with her past. But here was Brice, avoiding them, staying silent. *Coward.*

He set his toolbox on the table and faced her. "What…?" He waited until she glanced his way. "What could I have done? When I was a child. What could I have done to be good enough for you to care about me?" The words hurt coming out more than he'd imagined, like removing embedded burrs from skin.

She focused on a spot on the wall and waved her hand in a dismissive manner. "This is just the way life is."

"You didn't answer my question." He shouldn't push her, really he shouldn't, but at the same time, he needed to hear her reply. He'd never be able to heal until this conversation took place. "Why don't you like me? What…what could I have done differently…? How could I have made…?" His voice caught. *You love me.*

"Nothing. There is nothing you could have done." She blinked rapidly. "Every time I look at you, I see the life I could have had if I hadn't gotten pregnant with you." She looked down at the magazine. "My life would have been better. There were other men pursuing me. Men besides your father. But then you came along." She shrugged.

That's not my fault. I was only a child. He choked back the words racing through his mind. Saying them wouldn't help. He'd gotten his answer. Nothing. Nothing would have made him measure up. There was nothing he could accomplish that would make him good enough for her. Nothing he did would ever matter to her.

She scanned the room and heaved a sigh. "My life could have been so much better than this."

Brice grabbed the handle of his toolbox, letting the cold metal press hard against his hand. "You're right, Mom. Your life could have been better, but not how you think." She didn't look up, but he pressed on anyway. "See, you could have had a son who adored you, if only you'd allowed me to love you. But you didn't, and that has nothing to do with Dad." He pulled open the door but then glanced over his shoulder, waiting. If she asked for forgiveness, if she said she was sorry, he'd cross the room in three steps and hug her. But she wore a mask of indifference.

Brice rushed out to his car and jammed his key into the ignition. He drove home, hoping to find comfort in the solitude of his cabin. Instead he found loneliness. And one question pounded over and over in his head.

Would he ever matter—really matter—to anyone?

Kendall looped her arm through her friend Maggie West's and scanned the packed crowd at the Venetian Festival.

Freebie booths and an area with kids' games took up the left half of the parklike town square. The roses in the small garden that lined the far edge of the square were a riot of pink and yellow and red in full bloom. Fragrant flowers mixed with the delicious scent of fried goodies wafting from the food trucks parked around the square. Kendall might have to snag a fried Oreo later. Her mouth watered in agreement.

A performing group from one of the nearby colleges played swing-style dance music in the red band shell. Couples and young children danced near the gazebo under arches of hanging white Christmas lights. Teenagers lounged on the park benches, tossing candy at each other and snapping photos on their cell phones.

Kendall huddled in a group of local women made up of Maggie West, Paige and Shelby Beck, and Jenna Crest but continued to search the park benches and shadowed areas of the party for signs of Laura Daniels. After Brice's sister had stopped by for advice, Kendall felt the need to protect the girl from any more of Drew Foster's influence. In fact, Kendall had filled out a volunteer sheet at church during a midweek meeting to start serving in the youth group. If she could use her story, if sharing her mistakes and showing love to the teenagers in this community saved even one of them from following the same path she had, then being open with all of them would be worth it. But for now, if she spotted Laura getting cozy with the boy, she wouldn't hesitate to drag Brice's sister away. Even if that meant Laura disliking her.

But there were too many people at the event to spot familiar faces unless, as she'd done with her friends from Bible study, she picked a spot at the party to meet up at. Tourists spilled onto the bricked road around the square and filtered in and out of the art gallery, homemade fudge shop, ice-cream parlor and other stores that had extended their hours to stay open during the event.

Since it was the final night of the Venetian Festival and the sun was beginning to set, people were starting to make their way down to Ring Beach, which lay just off the square. The parade of decorated boats was set to start in the next half hour, and it would be followed by a small fireworks show. A string of bonfires on the beach, organized by the Goose Harbor Chamber of Commerce, drew people down to the sandy shore like bugs to a porch light.

Paige pointed at the beach. "We should stake out our spot near one of the fires before they get super crowded. I'm determined to roast the best marshmallow."

Jenna nodded. "The s'mores are always epic."

Kendall laughed. "How exactly can s'mores be more epic than they already are? I mean, it's pretty hard to top the amazingness that is melted marshmallows and chocolate."

Maggie nudged her in the ribs. "They have all kinds of extras you can add, like using peanut butter cups instead of chocolate or adding hazelnut spread, strawberries or caramel to them."

Paige groaned as she placed both her hands on her baby bump. "You guys sure know how to torture a pregnant lady. Now I want *all* of them."

Jenna threw her arms wide and hollered, "Make way for the hungry pregnant lady!" The nearby band drowned out her call, but the group of friends had a good laugh all the same. Shelby broke off from the group when she spotted her boyfriend, Joel, and Maggie ducked away as she spotted Kellen and his daughters near the water's edge playing in the sand. Kellen had set up a cooler and a blanket, saving his family a prime spot to view the fireworks.

Kendall grabbed Paige's arm, helping her walk steadily through the uneven patches of sand. Paige patted her arm and then glanced Jenna's way, smiling. "Guess you ladies are stuck with me. Caleb's down the beach playing flag football with a group of the high school boys."

Jenna jutted her chin in the direction of the football players. "He's already such a great teacher. He's going to be the best dad."

Paige wrapped her arms around both Kendall and Jenna. "I want you both to know that I pray for you daily. For both of you to feel pursued by the endless love of God, and I also pray for both of your future spouses. That God's preparing men who love Him above all else to be your husbands. I pray that the men who seek after your hearts one day will have spirits that are soft toward the Lord's will. You are both treasures. Don't settle for a man who doesn't cherish you."

Kendall's eyes burned as she held in tears. "Thank you," she whispered and squeezed Paige's arm before letting go.

For her whole life Kendall had dreamed of people caring about her—wished her mother would have bothered enough to guide her or her father had returned home. While she'd let go of the hope that either of those things would happen, here in Goose Harbor God had brought people into her life who were beginning to love her the way her family should have, people willing to speak into her life and offer a kind word when she appeared down. People like Paige, who had been praying for her without Kendall even asking her to. Had Kendall ever thought to pray for Paige, for anyone else? She would now.

Kendall focused on the flames of the bonfire as they pressed against the edging darkness of evening. Paige had known her for only a few months, and yet she was praying for Kendall's future husband. Kendall was speechless. When she first met Brice he'd mentioned how God had a way of answering prayers a person hadn't even prayed yet. Of blessing people with gifts they hadn't known to ask for.

"I...I have to go take care of something. See you both later?" Kendall stepped away from Paige and Jenna. She slipped out of her sandals and padded down to where the lake lapped peacefully on the edge of Ring Beach and then continued along the water until she was away from the crowd. She wiggled her toes into the wet sand. In one hand she clutched her sandals and the other she used to shield her eyes from the setting sun.

"Thank You," she quietly prayed. "I don't know why You keep giving me things I never thought I'd have. Friends. A hopeful career." A tear slipped down her cheek. "But thank You." It was all so much. So many blessings.

So much she didn't deserve.

It was impossible not to wonder when everything would come crashing down, because in Kendall's life, the crash was a given. There was still the possibility that her mother could ruin everything for her. If Sesser's partnership became public, her business would go belly-up and she'd never be able to pay him back. Her newfound friends were bound to realize that Kendall didn't belong in their group; they all seemed perfect, as if they never struggled at all. At some point they'd discover that Kendall didn't have it all together.

Then there was Brice. He was sweet and kind. While she enjoyed every minute she spent getting to know him, how long could their easy friendship last? Old lies crept into her mind, whispering that he would grow bored with her. That he would leave the way everyone always did.

Last but not least, Kendall didn't know what to think about God. While she believed in Jesus and was a Christian, she held God at arm's length. He didn't want to be involved in her life. Not on a personal, detailed level. That was what she had always thought. But if He was responsible for leading her to Goose Harbor and for her friendships here, how could she deny any longer that He cared about her as an individual?

If God cared like that…that sort of love had the power to change her entire life. Then again, even if she and God shared a moment of peace right now, even that could crumble if she did something wrong. Right? One incorrect step, one foolhardy decision, and God's blessing and love would vanish. And that was the scariest thought of them all. After feeling loved by God, losing His favor would be heart wrenching. That was how all of Kendall's relationships always seemed to go, so why would it work any differently with God?

But for now…for now she would savor the moment. During her interview with Jason she'd wondered if she had ever experienced a time when everything in her world was right—a memory worth cherishing. She'd foolishly only considered it in a romantic way, but this—right now—was her first perfect moment, and she'd cherish it, even though it would be gone by the time she tucked herself in bed.

Kendall sloshed a few inches deeper into the water, letting it tickle back and forth against her ankles. She hugged herself, fighting a shiver. The lake had cooled down by a surprising amount.

After a few minutes she let out a long breath. It was time to head back and join her friends. She turned around and spotted Paige cuddled next to her husband as they laughed with a group of high school students. Jenna appeared to be deep in conversation with an elderly lady as they roasted marshmallows together. Which was fine; Kendall didn't feel like returning to the party. She'd had enough large group interaction for one day. The condo she was renting was a short walk down the beach. Instead of navigating her way through the crowd on Ring Beach and in the town square to get back to her car parked near her office, she would just leave it parked in town and pick it up tomorrow.

A second before she resolved to follow through on her plan, she spotted Brice sitting on a bench at the end of the boardwalk. Not just any bench, their bench— the place they had sat together a few weeks ago when they shared ice cream. Had that really been that long ago? He was far enough away from the party where no one would bother him, but near enough to still see what was happening. As if a string tied her heart to his, Kendall felt a tug to go to him and her feet started in his direction before she'd even resolved to head over.

Hopefully he'd welcome her company.

Kendall cleared her throat as she approached the bench. While she knew that Brice wasn't a fan of large crowds, the slump of his shoulders told her there might be more going on than simply avoiding the people on the beach. Her bare feet slapped against the boardwalk. "Happen to have room for one more?"

Brice glanced her way. His lips pulled into a tight smile that didn't reach his eyes. "There's still a lot of the party left. I doubt you want to waste the rest of it sitting next to me."

Something was definitely wrong. Had she upset him? Or was his mood unconnected to her altogether?

She gripped her sandals a little firmer as she searched her mind, going over their last couple interactions. Nothing negative. In fact, he'd been acting more friendly than usual with her. Flirty even. Kendall took a tentative step closer. "Brice?"

He sighed. "You'll have a much better time if you head back to the bonfires and mingle with everyone." He jutted his chin toward the gathering crowd.

The campfire smell of wood popping under the heat of fire filled the air. With the sun close to setting, a chill had begun to creep across the beach. No matter how hot the day had been, Lake Michigan's presence kept the nights cool. A breeze whispered through the thin forest covering the top of a nearby dune. The wind carried into the crater of Ring Beach and washed over Kendall, sending a shiver down her back. In her shorts and tank top, she wasn't dressed for a drop in temperature.

She sat down on the bench and slid over to get closer to Brice, relishing the warmth of another person nearby. "How about you let me be the judge of where I want to be and who I'll enjoy spending my time with the most?"

Brice stared out toward the lake. The muscle in his jaw popped. Her fingers itched to touch his cheek. To make his stress disappear. But would that help him? She didn't know. What would be best? The answer came to her quickly: she should pray for him, as Paige had done for her.

Please. Please help me figure out what's bothering him. Give me the right words. The right questions. Let me be Your hands.

"Brice, what's going—"

"The boats are about to start." Over the past fifteen minutes vessels of every shape and size had begun to line up in the lake. Brice pointed toward them.

She laid her hand on his knee. "I think we should talk."

He shook his head. "It's your first Venetian Festival. Let's not ruin it. There'll be time to talk later."

Kendall swallowed hard but nodded. She wouldn't force him to share what was troubling him…at least not yet. The possibility loomed that whatever he was battling, he didn't want to share it with her. If that was the case, she'd have to respect his wishes.

He pressed his palms together and rubbed them back and forth as if he had sand coating his hands. "I'm sorry I didn't enter our paddle wheeler."

Was that the cause of his sudden distant attitude? Misplaced guilt over not using the parade to market their cruises? Silly man. If that was the reason for his mood, she could fix everything between them. Fix it so the peace she'd felt on the beach as she prayed carried into this moment with Brice.

"Not our boat. *Your* boat," she urged. "But between you and me, decorating the paddle wheeler and parading it around doesn't seem your style. And I'm glad you didn't enter it. Really glad actually."

He quirked an eyebrow and shifted to meet her eyes. "You are?"

"Of course." She bumped her shoulder into his. "If you were in the parade, then you couldn't be here with me. And I'd much rather have you beside me."

There. That should assure him. Everything would be all right.

Besides, they hardly needed more advertising. Papers and magazines were calling from places all over the Midwest for more information on her business. People were booking her date-planning services months in advance. She had some up-front payments stretching far into the Christmas season. The sunset cruises had been an instant success, so much so that the last two weeks they had to turn people away because the boat had reached capacity. Their clientele spanned tourists to anniversary couples to local teenagers taking each other on first dates.

A loud horn sounded and everyone on the beach started to cheer as they pressed closer to the shoreline. Kendall was sitting close enough to notice the muscles in Brice's arm and shoulder go rigid.

Why wasn't he relaxing?

A sick feeling rolled through her stomach. Somehow she'd made a mess of everything with him, hadn't she? Disappointed him in some way. Kendall blinked against the burn of tears.

Her mother's voice charged through her head. *Mark my words—he won't stick with you for long. You're too much like me, Kenny. Neither of us can keep a man.*

She scooted away from him on the bench.

A part of her wanted to jump to her feet and start running, run until the breath heaved from her lungs and all she could think about was her sore muscles. Run home. Close the door on all the ridiculous hopes she'd allowed to take root in her heart.

But her more rational side told her something else, something unrelated, was going on with Brice. He was struggling, and she needed to be here for him. Kendall couldn't let her old fears surrounding men and relationships get in the way of whatever was happening between her and Brice. She couldn't—wouldn't—lose his friendship. Because…truth be known, she didn't just want a friendship with this man any longer. She was falling for him and he deserved to know that.

A second horn sounded and all the boats lit up, soliciting applause from the event goers. The first boat chugged as close to the shore as it could. It was simply decorated with American flags and white Christmas lights. Goose Harbor's elderly mayor sat in a chair near the front, and the rest of the staff from city hall waved from on board.

The next boat had a sign proclaiming Goose Harbor Public Works. The side was decorated with orange construction signs reading Slow, Use Left Lane, Watch for Workers and Road Construction Ahead. Construction horses with blinking lights gave the boat a disco feel. All the men on board wore safety vests and hard hats and danced to "Y.M.C.A.," making the boat rock. They received a huge response from the crowd, who all laughed.

Kendall found it difficult to focus on the parade and near impossible to enjoy it amid the turmoil between her and Brice. *Tell him. Tell him now.* But Brice had been right to say they wouldn't be able to talk during the event; the crowd's murmurs along with music that accompanied each ship would have added further strain to a serious conversation.

The parade continued with boats of every size. The local drama troupe acted out a scene from Shakespeare's *The Tempest*, and a string of ships followed that had lights strung in ways to disguise the shapes of the boats. One looked like a semitruck floating on the water, another like a submarine, and yet another had different colored lights hanging in the shapes of palm trees. A ship toward the end of the line boasted a huge windmill. Clog dancers in full costume clomped to a lively tune. The final boat was lit to look like Cinderella's pumpkin coach from the fairy tales. A lady stood in the center blowing kisses to the crowd. Her blond hair was tucked back just like the famous princess's always was, and she wore the poufy blue signature dress.

The people on the beach all rose to their feet and clapped as the boats continued down to dock at the pier near the square. Everyone would be allowed to take turns getting an up-close view of all the boats, and there were ballots available so people could vote for the one they liked the most. But Kendall and Brice stayed on the bench.

Tell him you're falling for him.

If he didn't feel the same way, would that ruin their business relationship?

What was she going to do?

Brice ground his molars together. Kendall deserved answers. But sometimes words hurt on the way out, like the ones he'd had with his mother. His throat still felt raw from that exchange. He'd thought he would be out of sight this far down the beach…had expected Kendall to capture everyone's attention at the party as she did his. What he hadn't planned was that she'd leave the crowd and seek him out. Of course he wanted her nearby; that wasn't the issue. He still felt so raw and cut up from dealing with his mother that he didn't know what to do with those emotions and felt bad bringing down Kendall's fun night.

He watched her out of the corner of his eye. She'd moved away from him, leaving his side. With her arms wrapped around her stomach, she was either cold or upset.

He rubbed his palms over the worn fabric of his jeans. "I need to explain—"

"I…I…" Kendall's voice shook. "I should probably head home."

Brice hooked his hand around the back of his neck. "You aren't going to stay for the fireworks?" *Don't go.* But then, he hadn't given her much of a reason to remain. He knew he had been acting detached with her, but it wasn't because of Kendall. She needed to know that. If he could convince her to stay here with him—forever—he would.

She swiped at her eyes.

Wait. Was she crying?

Brice caught her by the arm as she made a move to stand. "Hey. Are those tears?" His gut twisted. *Buffoon.* He'd made her cry. "Kendall, what's wrong?" He mentally kicked himself for acting so coldly moments before.

"What's going on between us?" She ran her fingers under her eyes.

Oh. Not the response he'd expected. "I don't—"

She closed her eyes tightly. Then she opened her eyes, took a deep breath and said, "Did I ruin everything, all those nights ago, when I said I didn't want to date? Or is there still a possibility that you might want to take a chance on me?"

What? He leaned forward. "Of course I want you. I've wanted to date you since almost that first day. I didn't think you'd ever... You want to be with me?"

"Yes. Of course. But if you feel that way, why were you acting like you were?" She pushed her hands into her hair, winding chunks of it around her fingers, and pulled, making her hair stick up at odd angles.

She kept talking. "And don't say you weren't acting weird. I'm not overthinking all this. You were being strange. You still are." She pointed at him. "You didn't even want me to sit here with you. You didn't want me to stay—" Her voice broke again. "I'm sorry. You must think I'm being ridiculous."

He'd tried—tried very hard—to keep from being affectionate with her, but with Kendall doubting her place in his heart, he couldn't hold back any longer.

"Kendall," Brice groaned as he pulled her into his arms. She tucked her head into his chest so it fit right under his chin. "It's not like that. Not at all," he whispered into her hair and rubbed a circle against her back. She shivered in his arms. Brice loosened his hold on her and shrugged out of the zip-up hooded sweatshirt he was wearing. He draped it around her shoulders. "Here. You're freezing. Put this on."

"I'd hardly say freezing. But thanks." She slipped her arms into the sleeves and wrapped the extra fabric in the front of the sweatshirt so it doubled back around her sides.

They sat in silence for a minute before she broke it. "Brice? What's wrong?"

The first firework exploded above the lake, sending a flash of red across the waters. Brice examined Kendall by the light of the next two fireworks. With her almost black wavy hair, soulful brown eyes and dark complexion, Kendall Mayes was the most beautiful woman he'd ever seen. And she wanted to be with him. His heart pounded in his ears. "I'm sorry I was like that. I had a rough encounter with my mom today."

"Is she like mine?"

"You could say that."

"Whatever is going on in here—" she tapped his forehead "—don't believe it. Okay? Promise me you're not going to internalize whatever she said to you."

Kendall was so good. So kind. What had he done to deserve her in his life? Brice swallowed past his emotion. "Are you sure, about me and you? You haven't been in town very long."

Kendall pulled her feet up onto the bench and wrapped her arms around her legs. "For the record, I've been in town three months. I was here for six weeks before launching my business."

She'd yet to answer whether she was sure about him or not. "Still, that's not too long, and you've been busy most of the time you've been here."

"Fine, but what does that have to do with anything?" Her eyebrows lowered.

"You haven't met everyone in town yet." *Just say it.* "There are a lot of single men your age who you haven't met yet. Good guys. Guys who—"

"You're seriously telling me to go date other men?"

"No. I just want to make sure you're not disappointed with me later."

"Nothing I say is going to convince you that I've fallen for you. I see that now." Kendall shook her head, working her lip between her teeth for a second; then without warning she fisted her hands into his shirt and tugged him forward, pressing her lips to his. Fireworks popped and fizzed in the air as he worked his hands into her hair and she continued their kiss. She kissed him as if it might be the only kiss they would ever share and she wanted to pour all her feelings into it.

When they finally came up for air, Kendall wrapped her arms around him and positioned herself so her mouth was near his ear. "Don't ever, ever talk like that. Don't belittle yourself. Hear me? You're the best man I've ever met. Believe me."

Not trusting his voice, he swallowed hard and nodded.

"And we both have family issues we're dealing with. Maybe that's why we're a good fit. We both understand."

He hadn't forgotten. It was only that Kendall didn't seem as negatively affected by what she'd experienced in childhood. She wasn't shell-shocked about love like Brice still was.

"How do you do it?" Brice's voice came out hoarse. "How are you so positive and able to move on from all the injustice that happened to you?"

"I choose to forgive my mother, daily." She spoke softly. He had to lean closer to hear her over the sound of the fireworks show. "I have to. I'd be the most bitter person alive if I didn't."

Kendall had challenged him before about forgiving the people who had hurt him in his past. But could moving forward really be that easy? No. *Easy* was the last word he'd associate with the act of forgiveness. If Brice gave up the labels of being abused by his father, mistreated by his mother and rejected by Audra... who would he be? How could he define himself apart from the life circumstances that had shaped him into the person he was?

It was too much to consider. And right now he wanted to enjoy spending time with Kendall. He'd muddle through his thoughts on forgiveness another day. Or never. He glanced over at Kendall and smiled. Life seemed pretty okay right now.

Kendall leaned back against the bench and wove her fingers through his, and with her head snug against his shoulder, they watched the finale of the fireworks show, together.

Chapter Twelve

The *Chicago Tribune*.

Kendall's hands shook as she set the phone back in its cradle and jotted down the interview date and time. Love on a Dime was going to be featured in the travel section of the *Chicago Tribune*, which would bring in even more clients. Hiring an assistant would have to move up on her to-do list. She owed Claire's cousin Jason Moss a gift basket or at least a high five for all the attention his original article had brought in.

She couldn't wait to tell Brice.

Ever since their conversation at the Venetian Festival, he'd been treating her as if they were dating. Their friendship had turned into a relationship, and Kendall was loving every minute of it. Granted, it had been only four days, but they made up the best four days of Kendall's life. Brice dropped by her storefront each day, usually bringing a gift along. One day it was birthday cake fudge—which was possibly the best dessert she'd ever tasted—the next day it was fresh flowers to replace the dead ones in her vase, and another day he'd slyly left a handwritten note on her desk that she hadn't discovered until after he left. It had simply read "Miss you already."

And Brice thought he wasn't good with women. Kendall snorted.

"Well, that's not a very becoming noise." The sound of Claire Atwood's voice made Kendall jump. They both started to laugh. Claire winked at her. "Always nice to see you looking so happy."

Kendall had lost track of time. She reached over to grab her purse. Claire was stopping in to collect Kendall's bimonthly payment on her loan from Sesser.

"You too," Kendall said, indicating Claire's wide smile. "Every time I see you, you're all but glowing."

Claire's smile widened even more. "They do say new mothers have a glow." Warmth flooded her voice. "Speaking of which, I'm leaving for Russia next week."

"Next week! Already? That's so exciting."

"I know!" Claire clasped her hands together. "I can't wait to have Alexei home." She sat down, her eyes sparkling. "The agency says I may end up staying over there for a month or two because everything has to become official through the court system before we can travel back to America."

Kendall nodded, encouraging Claire to share as much as she wanted. "That makes sense."

Claire continued. "Needless to say, I won't be stopping by your shop for the payments during that time."

Originally Kendall had asked where she could drop off the payments every other week. She'd figured it would be easy to swing by Sesser's office. But Claire had insisted that she would rather visit Love on a Dime to pick up the checks.

"Like I said when we first worked out the details,

you never needed to stop by. I can mail the checks like I do all my other bills."

Claire leaned forward, the topaz jewels in her necklace shimmering under the store's lights. "I know that, but I wanted a reason to come in and visit with you."

"You never needed a reason." Kendall fought the urge to round the desk and hug Claire. If Kendall knew she would react well, she wouldn't have hesitated, but she and Claire still weren't close enough for impromptu shows of affection. Besides, Claire wore a linen suit coat with capris and heels; Kendall didn't want to wrinkle her outfit. Maybe one day, though. The woman sincerely wanted a friend. No different than Kendall.

"That's nice to know," Claire whispered, almost to herself.

Kendall ripped the business check out of its spiral book and handed the paper to Claire. "Here's this week's check."

Claire's eyes went wide. "This is five times the agreed-upon payment amount."

"Business is going well. Much better than I ever could have imagined. I'd like to pay your dad back faster than the contract terms if I'm able to."

Claire tucked the check into her purse and then stretched across the desk to squeeze Kendall's hand. "I'm really proud of you. You know that, right?"

"Thank your dad for making me come up with a weekly event. I would never have thought to do that, but that has been one of the best decisions for my business. The sunset cruises that Brice and I run bring in enough to pay back your father without even touching the money I've been making from actual date planning."

"I'll be sure to let him know."

After Claire left, Kendall straightened up the office and recorded a new message on the business voice mail letting people know she'd be gone the rest of the day but would continue to check the missed calls. Her last call before locking the doors was to confirm a time of delivery with the caterer for tonight's sunset cruise rental.

Sweat gathered on the back of Kendall's neck as she loaded her car with the box of twinkle lights, freshly washed tablecloths, flowers and fancy dishes and then headed the short distance to the nice pier just off Goose Harbor's town square. Brice had arranged for her to leave her car behind a café near the pier where she'd have an ensured spot and no one would have a reason to tow it. Little, thoughtful things like that made Brice an amazing person. He considered details and took care of them without being asked.

A group of seagulls cawed as they strutted near the wooden pier looking for handouts. Within seconds a tourist situated on a bench tossed half of a sandwich their way. Breaking into a total frenzy, the gulls launched at the bun, turning it into nothing more than a crumb. In the water, hundreds of boats bobbed in unison, making it look as if they were all dancing to a secret melody. The sweet smell of waffle cones baking drifted through the air, making Kendall wish she had left a couple minutes earlier so she could have stopped at the ice-cream shop and picked up a cone for her and Brice to share.

Hot, late-July sun beat down on Kendall as she began to unload her car. She positioned the box of lights on her hip and looped a few bags onto her free arm. She'd have to make a couple trips back and forth to gather everything, but thankfully she'd stowed a change of clothes in her car on her way to work this morning. She'd be able to change in the paddle wheeler's bathroom and freshen up before Joel and Shelby's booked date.

Brice must have been watching for her, because she had made it only a few steps before she spotted him jogging down the pier. He cut across the grass that separated them and eased the heavy box from her grip. Then he leaned in and gave her a quick peck on the lips. It didn't last long enough.

He pressed his forehead to hers for a second and whispered, "It's good to see you."

She swatted at his chest. "You saw me this morning. Remember? When you dropped off coffee?"

"Of course I remember." He took the bags from her hands. "How could I forget seeing the prettiest woman in Michigan?"

Kendall bit the corner of her cheek, never knowing how to respond to his open flattery. She knew he was complimenting her in earnest because Brice was only ever genuine. But that almost flustered her more than if he had been joking with her. She had endured a lifetime of hearing the worst about herself from her mother. Nothing had prepared her to hear Brice's open praise.

She blew her bangs out of her eyes. "Enough of that. We've got work to do, mister. We have two hours to turn your boat into a dream date destination."

"Aye-aye, Captain." Brice winked at her. "You go start fancying up the boat and I'll carry over the rest of the stuff from your car."

"Deal." She circled back to the car and fished out her dress and heels.

They spent the next hour working side by side, stringing lights, hanging lanterns and setting up the table. At times they joked, and sometimes they were silent; either way, Kendall enjoyed every minute of time spent with Brice. He hummed as he straightened a lantern that was askew and leaned down to press a kiss to her temple as he passed on his way to go change into nicer clothes downstairs.

Kendall stopped what she was doing and watched him until he was too far down the stairs to see. She couldn't help the smile pulling at her lips. They were a team, her and Brice. An amazing team. Somehow, God had taken a man who preferred to be alone and a girl who said the first thing that popped into her head, and He'd brought them together and they worked. Brice seemed to be able to read her mind and he took care of her. She wanted to make sure she was doing the same for him.

She wouldn't lose him, not like all her other relationships. Meeting Brice had changed her, changed her life. She never wanted to go back to being the person she was before meeting him.

Never before had she imagined herself marrying any of the men she had dated or met in her past. She couldn't say that about Brice. It might be jumping too far ahead, but Kendall wanted to be with this man for the rest of her life.

Brice sucked in a breath. Would he forever be caught dumbfounded by the sight of Kendall Mayes in a dress?

He sure hoped so.

She waited on the pier, the light lake breeze tugging the black fabric around her knees and causing her to touch her hairstyle—what she called a messy bun but Brice thought looked nothing but perfect—a couple times to make sure the wind hadn't yanked any of her hair loose from the binding. It took everything in him not to cross the boat, pull her toward him and kiss her again.

But she'd told him to behave. They were working right now. This was Joel and Shelby's date, not theirs. However, she had winked when she said the word *behave*, so his attention didn't bother her. If the evening went well, they'd be able to sneak in some time together on the boat after Joel and Shelby left. Maybe Brice would even be able to convince Kendall that they should take the boat back out on the lake again and count the stars, just the two of them.

Joel and Shelby arrived on time. Joel led Shelby blindfolded down the pier. He smiled toward Brice and Kendall but spoke to his girlfriend. "Easy. Five more steps."

"Joel, honestly…where are you taking me?" Shelby laughed.

Kendall held the gate on the paddle wheeler open as Joel lifted Shelby over the gap between the boat and the pier and carried her toward the table. Shelby squealed, but even with her blindfolded, her arms found a safe place immediately around Joel's neck. When Joel finally told her to take off the blindfold, Shelby yelped loudly and sprang from her chair.

She dropped onto Joel's lap and bear-hugged him. "I can't believe you planned all this."

Joel ran his hand over her hair. "I might have had some help." He waved toward Brice and Kendall.

Kendall stepped forward with appetizers—some sort of hard bread covered in tomatoes—in hand. "Pretend we're not even here."

Brice started the paddle wheeler and maneuvered the vessel out onto the lake. Even though Goose Harbor was a bustling tourist town, it took only a few minutes to navigate deep enough into the water to suddenly feel as if they were the only people for miles. That was what had originally attracted Brice to the shipping industry—the pull of being able to get away from the crowds, yet still live in his hometown. Joel had let Kendall know that he wanted the boat ride to feel intimate, so Brice continued the route, taking the paddle wheeler deeper and deeper. By sunset, they'd be completely isolated.

The night continued as planned. Joel and Shelby both raved about the food. They watched the sunset while holding on to each other and then swayed together when Kendall turned on music. After the fourth song Kendall lowered the music and let them know their time was coming to a close. She signaled for Brice to start the engine.

Joel turned toward Kendall. "Thank you for planning all this. We had a great time."

"Wait." Shelby tugged out of his arms. "We're heading back? Now?" She swiped at her eyes. "But I thought…I thought…" She covered her face with her hands.

Joel shot an alarmed look Brice's way. "Shelb? Sweetheart." He set his hands on her shoulders. "What's wrong? I thought you had a good time. Talk to me."

She shrugged away from his touch. "I thought you

were bringing me out to propose." Her voice rose. "I kept waiting. I…I'm so stupid."

Kendall took a step forward and froze. She glanced over at Brice with a *what should I do?* look on her face. Brice grimaced back. How could Shelby be acting the way she was? Joel had spent a lot of money to take her out on a nice date. And she cried? It didn't make sense. Brice's gut clenched. The whole situation reminded him of Audra. But Shelby wasn't like Audra at all. Brice had known her his whole life, since they both grew up in Goose Harbor. There had to be something else going on.

Joel stumbled backward. "You thought I was going to propose?"

"Apparently that's a shocking thought." Shelby cried harder. "I need a minute to myself. Don't follow me." She took off down the stairs.

Joel looked at the stairs and then made eye contact with Brice, then Kendall. He raked his hand through his hair. "I don't… What just happened?"

Kendall held up her hand. "Don't worry. I'll take care of her." She took the stairs down two at a time, leaving Brice alone to deal with Joel.

"Tough break." Brice cut the engine.

"I have no idea what went wrong." Joel turned pleading eyes on him. "I love her. That's what tonight was about. To celebrate the fact that we've been together for a year. But…" He let out a long stream of air.

"She's acting on emotion. Without thinking. There's probably something else going on or something she's struggling with that she hasn't talked to you about yet." Brice pushed on, even though Joel might not want to hear what he had to say. "More than anything, she needs your grace right now. That is, if you love her and want to stay with her after tonight."

"If I want to… Of course I want to stay with her." Joel jerked back his head as if he found the thought of breaking up with Shelby repulsive. "Didn't you hear me say I love her? Love doesn't walk away from a misunderstanding. Love perseveres. I learned that lesson early in our relationship. I'm going to wait over there for her." He pointed at a chair near the railing. "I'm going to pray for her while Kendall talks to her."

Brice nodded, knowing he'd been dismissed. He weighed what he should do but decided to head downstairs, hoping to help talk some sense into Shelby. If anything, he could assure her about how much Joel loved her.

Brice padded down the steps, not wanting to interrupt the women if they were at a sensitive part of their conversation. If it didn't sound as though he was needed, he'd swing around and head back upstairs. He froze behind the partition that separated the stairs from the lower part of the boat.

Shelby sucked in a shaky breath. "I know I overreacted. I'm just having a hard time. We've been dating for a year. He keeps saying that he wants to spend the rest of his life with me but then never proposes. What if he never asks, Kendall? What do I do?"

"Have you talked to him about what sort of timeline you'd like for marriage?" Sensible Kendall. She'd make things right.

"No." Shelby paused. "He…he hasn't brought it up, and I know for as much as he loves me, the thought of being married scares Joel. He grew up in foster care, so he never really got to see a functioning family. I think he's terrified of doing something wrong." Brice pulled at his collar as Shelby kept talking. "But I don't get it. Doesn't he realize that he's not the type of person his mother or father were? He's going to be an amazing husband."

"I hear you. But I understand Joel's feelings too." Kendall spoke with a quiet assurance in her tone. "I grew up with a single mom. My dad left when I was really young. I've been terrified of being abandoned by a man ever since. Then I met Brice, who is so wonderful, and he doesn't even realize it because he's worried about repeating his family's mistakes, as well. I think we all carry fears from our childhood with us into adulthood. It's hard not to."

Brice braced his hands against the wall. Kendall was right. He was worried about repeating his family's mistakes. He'd allowed worry to almost destroy his chance with Kendall.

Shelby groaned. "But I don't want to date forever. I want to be married. To Joel. Why doesn't he get that? What more am I going to have to do to prove that I'm not going to leave him or abandon him? Not ever."

"Be honest with him," Kendall urged. "These things you're saying right now, say to him."

"Thanks, Kendall. You know, when I heard Kellen took Maggie out on a cruise and proposed, I struggled with jealousy. They haven't been dating long—a couple months! And he proposed right away. Maggie will probably be married and back from her honeymoon before Joel even starts to think about proposing."

"You need to talk to Joel about that too—how you struggled over the news about Kellen and Maggie. If he's the man you want to marry, if you're serious about the relationship, then there shouldn't be secrets like that between you two. You need to be open and trust him with things like that, things that hurt."

Brice slowly put his foot back on the steps. The women didn't need his input. And overhearing more truth might overwhelm his brain. He had to start communicating with Kendall—completely open and honest—the same as she was asking Shelby to do with Joel. He had to tell her how much he struggled with the things his mom said to him. Tell her his fear of feeling powerless and out of control. Admit the anger he still harbored against Sesser Atwood. Kendall had to know all those things about him.

"You're right. I feel so foolish now. Poor Joel. He planned this whole romantic evening for me and I ruined it."

"I don't think he'll see it that way. He loves you, Shelby. That's as plain as the hair on his head."

Shelby laughed. "He's head over heels. I am too. I need to go up there and make things right."

Brice padded back up the stairs and got into position behind the steering wheel. Hopefully the women hadn't heard him.

Chapter Thirteen

Kendall glanced over at Brice as he led her down the boardwalk toward a less-populated stretch of the beach. Tourists might flood Ring Beach every day throughout the summer, but the dune grass worked like fencing against them for the most part. They stayed on the famed Ring Beach and left the rest of the shoreline to the locals.

"All right." Kendall nudged Brice in the ribs with her elbow. "What's with all the secrecy?" He'd called her at the office earlier and asked if she could close an hour ahead of her normal time. When she'd consented, he said he would pick her up for a date and wouldn't give her any details.

"No secrecy here." He raised his hands in mock surrender. "Can't a man want to spend time with his favorite person?"

"I *guess* that's a good enough reason." She looped her arm through his, letting him set a slow pace as they headed in the direction of the old lighthouse that marked the border where Goose Harbor met the town of Shadowbend. With each step the wooden planks beneath their feet groaned. The side of the boardwalk closest to the beach was sandy, and tall dune grass waved—an ocean in its own right—on the other side of the walkway. Dunes rose beyond the grassy patches, sandy until the tops, which sprouted with a thin line of trees. Staircases were built into a few of the nearby dunes, heading to private homes in the wealthiest section of town.

Brice guided her down the beach for another ten minutes until he pointed to a blue tarp tucked around a pile of items closer to the water. The stuff was situated near one of the park district installed fire-pit sites, so there was a built-in, safe area to cook.

"I came out here earlier and dropped this stuff off."

Kendall helped Brice pull back the tarp. "Good thing a bear didn't find it first." Her gaze took in the large cooler, flannel blanket and pile of firewood. "Wait. Are there bears in this part of Michigan?" She glanced back toward the tree line. They were awful close to the forest if bears were a threat, not to mention they were remote too. If something happened, no one would hear them yell.

Brice gently tugged the tarp out of her hold as he chuckled. "While there is a strong black-bear population in Michigan, at least ninety percent of them live in the upper peninsula. I think we're safe." After he tucked the tarp into a large bag, he grabbed two edges of the blanket and flung it out so it spread across the grass. Tugging the cooler over, he used its weight to keep the blanket down.

Kendall lowered herself onto the blanket and opened up the cooler, peeking inside. She made eye contact over the top of the cooler's lid. "And what about the other ten percent of the black bears?"

Brice arranged the chopped wood under the cooking grate of the fire pit, tucking kindling—which happened to be dryer lint—between the cracks. "They'll probably join us for dinner."

"Brice!" She leaned around the cooler and swatted his shoulder. "I'm being serious."

"You have nothing to be worried about. Most of that ten percent stays up in the northern portion of the hand of Michigan. We get a sighting of one every few years. Nothing more." He lit the fire and spent the next ten minutes coaxing the flames to take over the wood.

"So dryer lint, huh?"

"Little-known fact, it makes the best kindling. Goes up at a high temperature." He shrugged. "And easily available."

Kendall pulled cups and plates and little Tupperware containers from the cooler. One had cubed cheese. Another had grapes. Still another container held what appeared to be the most mouthwatering chocolate layer cake Kendall had ever seen. In a large plastic zip baggie, Kendall located two huge items wrapped in foil.

"Oh, good." Brice eased the foil packs from her hands. "You found the salmon." He tossed them onto the grate that covered the fire pit.

Over the next half hour Brice flipped the salmon a couple times while Kendall lay back, hands behind her head, watching the clouds inch across the sky on their way to tuck the sun into bed. Her clothes and hair would smell like wood smoke when she got back home, and she would love it. Somehow the smell made her think of Brice, even though this was their first campfire meal together. Rustic and manly, it suited him. There was no doubt it would be the first of many times sharing food over an open flame. Kendall smiled, comforted by the thought—by this life she was carving out in Goose Harbor.

When Brice declared the fish ready to eat, he opened both foil packs, arranging the salmon and vegetables beside the cheese and fruit. He said grace for their meal and they dug in.

Not sure what to expect tastewise, Kendall took her first bite. Notes of citrus, seasoning and something tangy she couldn't quite place burst on her tongue. "Wow." She took another bite. "This is so good. How did you make it?"

"It's been marinating in a mix of lemon, olive oil, salt, pepper and dill."

"Dill! That's the tangy part."

"It's the secret ingredient." He sent a wink her way before polishing off the rest of his vegetables.

Kendall gathered their empty dishes and piled everything back into the cooler. She patted her stomach. "That's the best meal I've had in a long time. I'm afraid I'm not much of a cook."

Brice touched the spot beside him on the edge of the blanket, facing the water. "Come sit beside me."

She gladly cuddled up next to him. He pulled the remaining blanket up to drape over their shoulders and then slipped his arm around her back. Kendall snuggled closer, breathing in the woodsy scent of him as she leaned her head against his side.

"This is my favorite spot." Kendall sighed.

"Watching the sunset?"

"Well, that's nice too." She tilted her head to better

look at him, making eye contact. "But I meant being beside you. Right here." She placed her hand on his chest and leaned closer, stealing a quick kiss before whispering, "You're my favorite place." Her heart thundered. It felt like such a bold statement to say out loud, but it was true.

He pressed his lips to her forehead and then eased her so she was facing the sunset again. "I really admired how you went down and talked to Shelby yesterday. How you encouraged her to mend her relationship with Joel."

Kendall gripped the edge of the blanket, pulling it tighter around herself. "When two people love each other they should be willing to work through the hardest parts together. I've come to the realization that that's what love is all about, sticking around through the really tough stuff. Saying you still believe in someone, even when they accidentally hurt you. That's love."

"Not planning a campfire date for a pretty lady?" He leaned into her, his tone letting her know he was joking.

She leaned back against him. "That part's nice too. Better than nice. This—you planning all this—was wonderful. Thank you."

"I'm sorry it wasn't impressive." He scrubbed his free hand over his jaw. "It's probably pretty simplistic compared to the dates you're hired to orchestrate."

"This one was better than all those."

"Really?" He angled his body to look down at her.

"Yes, because you didn't need help. *You* planned it all on your own. That counts more to me. I don't need extravagant, Brice. I just want time with you." She laced her fingers through the fringe on the edge of the blanket.

"And besides, there's something about our relationship and sunsets that goes hand in hand. Don't you think?"

Kendall was getting way ahead of herself, but she'd already considered what a wedding to Brice would look like. That should scare a commitment-phobic person such as herself, but with Brice, it didn't. She'd rent a portion of the beach and wear a flowy white dress. Her hair would be down her back, styled in loose curls, with only a crown of woven flowers for decoration. They'd both be barefoot, of course, and the ceremony would be perfectly timed so that when the minister pronounced them man and wife, the sun would be dipping below the horizon.

"I think of you every time the sun sets," he whispered. "Other times too. But sunsets are special. They're yours."

"Ours," she whispered back. "They're ours."

"You can't do this." Brice ground the words between his teeth. "You can't do this to us."

Sesser Atwood cleared his throat on the other end of the phone. "Actually I can."

The pencil in Brice's hand snapped in two. *Calm down.* He gaped at the broken pieces, letting them fall onto the office desk in the shipping warehouse. *Wars aren't won by losing your head.* He pushed out of his chair, yanking the phone close to the edge to give the cord enough room for him to stand.

There had to be a way to fight Sesser on this. Even if Brice had to gather the rest of the renters on the dock and seek legal counsel together, he'd do it. He would even be willing to foot the bill.

He clapped a hand over his forehead and jammed the

tips of his thumb and middle fingers into his temples. Brice took a shaky breath. "I signed a contract in order to move my boat to your downtown pier. A yearlong contract. It said—"

Sesser's loud, gravelly voice overtook Brice's words. "It said you can't back out of your year contract is what it said."

"I'm not backing out," Brice growled.

"Sure sounds like you want to." Was that…a laugh?

Breathe. Speak rationally. "That contract also states that the monthly charge for docking would stay the same for the twelve-month term."

"You're right. It does say that."

"So you're the one breaking contract."

"Your docking fee remains the same. The new fee is a tourist tax. A simple set amount for every passenger who boards your boat. Every single time you sail."

"But that's what I'm saying. You can't alter the contract terms."

"Flip over to article six in the contract papers and you'll see that I can."

Brice bit down hard, pressing his molars together, sending pain shooting throughout his jaw. A headache wasn't far off. With the way the day was playing out, it would probably become a full-blown migraine before noon.

Sesser filled the pause. "Now, if you need to break contract over this, remember I'll need the equivalent of nine months of docking fees up front. That's stated plainly in the paperwork you signed."

The tycoon had Brice trapped. It felt as if he'd been tossed onto burning coals and Brice's only choice was to dance along or go up in flames. It raked him to feel so out of control.

Showing weakness, being vulnerable with Sesser, was the equivalent of covering himself in raw meat and lying down amid a pack of wolves. But Brice had to know. "Why do you hate us? The Daniels family. What did we ever do to you?"

"Son—"

"I'm no son of yours," Brice snapped. His biological dad might have been an abusive gambler, but at least he didn't see every person in the world as someone to misuse for financial gain. No one was worse than Sesser Atwood. No one. Not even his father, Mason Daniels.

"I'm a businessman. I don't have room for hate."

Brice steadied his hand on the windowsill. "Or any other emotion, it would seem. Only money. It's all you care about."

"Your brother runs a business out of a storefront he rents from *me*." Sesser spoke in a calm but authoritative tone. "All of your ships are on *my* ports. And your pathetic parents may own that joke of a home now, but *I* still own all the land surrounding their house. I also hear your sister wants to find a part-time job, but one word from me and no business in town will hire her— let alone engage in business with you or your brother. Do you really want to challenge me?"

Everything Sesser said was true—the man had that much power. Brice really should bite his tongue, but he was so tired of keeping his head down. So weary from all the times in life he hadn't been able to defend himself, let alone the people he cared about.

Someone had to put Sesser in his place. "Threaten

to get your way. That's all you know how to do, isn't it? If Claire knew about—"

"Oh, I don't think you'd dare go down that road."

The door to his office creaked and Brice spun around, ready to glare at whoever from his crew happened to be interrupting him, but his hard look landed on Kendall. She froze and her smile faltered. A bag from Candy's Donuts dangled in her hand.

Brice held up a finger and mouthed, *One minute.* Then he faced the small window in his office again. He had to end the conversation with Sesser. Arguing was pointless because they were never going to see eye to eye. "Thanks for letting me know about the change in the contract, but listen here—if *I* have any changes I want to make to my end, I'll let you know by the end of the week."

"Always a pleasure doing business with you, Mr. Daniels."

"Wish I could say likewise."

When he turned around to hang up the phone, he found Kendall waiting on the other side of his desk. She'd set the bag of donuts down. "You've stopped by and surprised me every day this past week, so I thought I'd return the favor today. It sounds like I might have come at a bad time."

"It's a fine time." He rubbed his hand over his short hair.

"Brice." She laced her fingers together. "I didn't mean to listen in. And I honestly didn't hear much. But I've never heard you speak in that tone. What's wrong?"

"The dock owner found a way to rob me of all our earnings. Effective on Friday he's placed a tax on the head of every person I bring on board our sunset cruises."

"A tax? I don't understand."

"Somehow he's caught wind of how successful we've been and now he wants a cut of the pie." Brice sighed. "It's backhanded and unethical, but I'm afraid that's how Sesser Atwood works."

"Sesser Atwood? What does he have to do with this?"

Oh, right, Kendall was friends with Sesser's daughter. Brice tried to infuse gentleness into his voice. "Sesser owns both docks. I pay him for every boat I have to have there. Well, that was him on the phone. He's going to cut into our profit deeply if he really is allowed to enforce the tax."

Kendall dropped into the chair on the other side of his desk. She opened her mouth and then closed it, then opened it again. "Wait. Sesser owns the docks?"

Why was that so hard to comprehend? He nodded.

She rocked to the edge of the seat. "No problem, then. I'll speak to him. I'm sure he'll waive it for you. He must not realize we're in business together."

Why was Kendall speaking as though she was friends with Sesser? Brice's head pounded. "What are you talking about?"

She licked her lips and lowered her voice. "Will you promise not to tell anyone if I tell you something?"

"Okay." He drew out the word, not sure he wanted to make the promise she was asking of him, but agreeing anyway.

"Sesser is my secret business partner. He financially backed Love on a Dime. I know if I go speak with him he'll be more than happy to—"

"Your *what*?" Brice's voice rose. He couldn't help it. His mind had taken a moment to catch up to her words, but now they sank in. Sourness crept up the back of his throat. Kendall had a partnership with Sesser Atwood…the man he disliked most in the entire world.

"Partner." She looked down.

"No." The word came out hoarse, as if it had been ripped from his lungs. "That man…" He shook his head. "You can't be partners with him."

Kendall tipped her head back, her deep, soulful eyes meeting his. They reminded him of a sad animal, begging to be let in from the rain. *Look away.* He couldn't afford to go soft. Not when it had to do with Atwood. Not after all that man had done to the Danielses.

"He's been good to me," Kendall pleaded. "He—"

"I don't want to hear it." Brice held up his hand. Blood rushed through his veins like a freight train. "Is there a way to get out of the partnership?"

"There's not." She lifted her chin. "And I don't want out. I wouldn't have a business without him. I wouldn't know *you* without him."

"I owe that man nothing. Not. One. Thing." Brice shoved away from his desk and stalked to the window. "You have to break the partnership, Kendall."

"I can't."

"For me. Please? Can you do this for me?"

"I can't." Her bottom lip quivered.

Brice shoved his hand against the back of his head. "It's him or me. Don't you understand that? I can't be with you—not in a business deal or in a personal way—if you have a connection to that man."

"Where is this coming from? Talk to me, Brice. You're scaring me."

Brice pivoted and stalked toward her. "That man has ruined the lives of everyone I've ever cared about. He's held back my business for years. He uses, crushes and discards people. How can you even consider staying with him?"

"It's just business. Brice…look at me."

One clipped laugh burst from his lips. "You told Shelby that she shouldn't keep secrets from Joel, and here you were keeping this whopper of a secret from me. I trusted you, Kendall." His voice broke. Brice swallowed hard, regrouping. "I thought… It doesn't matter what I thought. You're not going to break your partnership with him, are you?"

A few tears slipped down her cheeks as she shook her head. "My business is gone if I do."

Kendall's confirmation hit with the pain of a crowbar against knees. He wanted to sink to the ground and crawl into a closet. Hide the way he had done when he was a child.

Worthless. No one wants you. No one would ever choose you. He wasn't good enough for her. He would never be good enough. Never be the one chosen. Women always picked the man with money. Just like Audra. How had he allowed himself to be blindsided again? Sure, there was nothing romantic between Sesser and Kendall, but that hardly mattered. She was still choosing to align herself with the man.

Brice crossed his arms over his chest, pressing against the hurt boiling inside. "He's my enemy, Kendall. How do you not get that?"

"Enemy? Really? Listen to yourself." She dashed tears away. "You sound like you're still in high school!"

"Out." Brice pointed toward the door. For her own

good, he had to get her to leave. He didn't want to say something he'd regret later. He had to think first. Had to piece his life together alone. Like always.

"Brice, you don't—"

"I don't want to talk to you right now. I can't. Please go." He sank back into his chair and rested his head in his hands. She hadn't moved yet. "Go."

"I will." She sounded as if she was choking back a sob. His heart squeezed. The logical part of his brain told him to go comfort her, to end the argument by taking her in his arms. But he quashed that thought by shoving his arms into his chest harder.

Her feet shuffled against the concrete floor. "But this conversation isn't done. Call me whenever you're ready. I'll wait. I'll always wait for you."

Emotions churned in his chest. *Chase after her!* But he kept his head down until he was sure she was gone.

Brice dug his cell phone out of his pocket and tore off the back. He yanked out the battery and tossed it into a nearby drawer. No one would be able to reach him. *Good.* He should have stayed an island. Should have kept to his cabin. Well, he'd learned his lesson good and hard now.

He'd never venture outside himself again.

Chapter Fourteen

Two days.

Kendall paced the length of her condo.

No one had seen or heard from Brice in two days. The men at the shipping warehouse hadn't sounded concerned when she dropped by looking for him the day following their argument. They said Brice was taking a few days off. No return date, at least not one they were sharing.

She dropped down into her eggplant-colored chair, scooping up her phone. Kendall swiped the screen, bringing it to life. But…she couldn't call him. Not without making herself look completely pathetic. She set the phone back on the coffee table. The first day she'd left him four messages. *Four.* And he hadn't returned her calls. The second day she'd called his phone three different times throughout the day and it still went straight to voice mail.

He obviously didn't want to be reached. And he obviously didn't want her.

She'd slipped up. Fallen for him. That hadn't been part of her plan. When it came to men, she'd always jetted before they had the chance, and this was why. Falling with no one waiting to catch her hurt. The pain now was different than when she was the little girl who had ached to know her father. Kendall felt a searing tear in her heart from loving a man who didn't want her.

She rubbed her thumb over the corduroy-like fabric on the armrest.

Men abandoned. Hadn't her mother drilled that into her head? Dad left, none of her mother's boyfriends had stuck around long and none of the men Kendall had dated had ever fought to keep her. She had thought Brice was different. Kendall pressed her palm into the place near her heart that throbbed. But Brice wasn't any different than the rest of them. When things got hard, she wasn't worth staying for.

Enough tears. She sucked in a shuddering breath. As long as Brice kept her partnership with Sesser a secret, she still had her business. And wasn't that the whole reason why she'd moved to Goose Harbor to begin with? Kendall wasn't made to be loved and cherished. She was gifted at helping others feel that way. Seeing the joy her planning brought to other people's lives, that would have to be enough for her from now on.

A knock sounded on her front door. Kendall had closed her office for the day, deciding to take a day or two to regroup, so she wasn't expecting anyone. She rose to her feet, padded over to the mirror on the wall and tried to swipe away her smudged makeup. The bags under her eyes made her grimace, but it would have to do.

She grabbed the door handle but then froze for a

moment. What if it was Brice? No...she couldn't get her hopes up. She had to move forward without thinking about him. He'd given her an ultimatum—cut ties with Sesser or cut ties with him—that wasn't okay. Even if Brice returned, would she ever be able to trust him again? Believe that he wouldn't just up and leave the next time they argued?

She eased open the door. Not Brice. A middle-aged man with a graying widow's peak, tan skin and a kind smile stood there. "Kenny?" His voice held a trace of awe.

Weird. No one besides her mother called her Kenny. Was this a new boyfriend? A way for her mother to deliver a message without causing problems with the police? Kendall bristled and inched the door so it was open by only a foot.

"I'm sorry—do I know you?" She started to close the door farther.

He cocked his head, kind smile still in place. "You don't remember me at all, do you?"

"I have no idea who you are."

"You were so young." He shook his head in a sad manner. "I'm your father, Kendall. It's me."

She yanked the door open all the way. "My...what?"

"I read about you in the paper. About your business." He pulled a sheet of newspaper from his back pocket and unfolded it carefully. "I've been searching for you for so many years. I'd started to give up hope of ever finding you." He passed her the news article.

She took the page but didn't look down at it. Her father? She didn't know whether she should hug him or slam the door in his face. This was the man who had left her first. The man who had started the pattern of abandonment.

"If you're my father, I don't know why you're here." With so much swirling in her mind, she didn't have the ability to rein in her words. "You left us. You walked out on me."

"I wouldn't have done that." His gaze raked over her face as if he was trying to memorize all her features. "I was filing for full custody. I wanted you—wanted to raise you."

But it didn't measure up. She narrowed her eyes. Her mother said he left. And he'd never returned—never come home or sought Kendall out before—so her mother had to be telling the truth, right? Then again, Mom wasn't known for *the whole truth and nothing but*. Kendall wasn't certain what to think.

"That's not true," Kendall mumbled.

"The day she took you…" His voice caught. He cleared his throat. "When I came home and found you, her and all your belongings gone…it felt like I was going to die." He shuffled his feet. "I didn't know where she took you, but I promise, I tried to find you. Even after the police closed the case and stopped searching. Even when my friends told me to move on. I've never stopped searching."

Kendall pressed her hand over her forehead. "Do you want to come in?" She motioned toward her small couch.

They spent the next two hours catching up. He explained how he and her mom hadn't even been dating when they found out they were expecting a baby. They tried to make a relationship work for her sake, but soon after Kendall was born, he caught her mother cheating on him. Since they were unmarried and hadn't sorted custody out in court yet, when her mother took off with Kendall the authorities didn't consider it kidnapping. It wasn't a crime for a mother to move with her child. Not unless there were court documents stating the father's visitation rights or granting full custody.

He'd hired investigators, but he had assumed they'd stayed in the state. But her mother had moved them out of Utah—Kendall's birth state—and they'd lived in ten different states in less than four years until they finally settled in the foothills of Kentucky when Kendall was five. Even then, they rarely stayed at the same address for long.

No wonder her father hadn't been able to track them.

"I married a few years after you went missing," her father said. "We moved to Ohio not long after that. It's hard knowing you were only a state away that whole time." He rocked forward, his elbows resting on his knees. "You have three siblings. They would really love to meet you."

Kendall had a family—people who had searched for her and longed to know her. "I have siblings?"

"Two brothers and a sister. They all live a few hours' drive from here, at most."

"You searched for me?" Kendall repeated for the seventh time. It was hard to rewire her thinking. Hard to realize the foundation of her beliefs concerning herself and what she thought about men was a complete lie.

"I've never stopped." His wife had shown him an article about Love on a Dime, originally suggesting that Goose Harbor looked like a nice place to go for a long weekend. But Kendall's name was mentioned in the article, and while her father knew there could be other women in the world named Kendall Mayes, he wasn't going to rest until he knew one way or the other.

"Kendall, I've loved you since the moment I knew you existed. So many years have been stolen from us, but if you're willing, I'd like to be a part of your life now."

Kendall had never been abandoned. She'd always been wanted. And now a family waited to meet her and be a part of her life. She leaned back in her chair. It was almost too much to believe. But it was true.

"I'd like that, Dad." She tried out the word to see how it felt. A peace Kendall had never known before settled over her soul.

Usually being in the woods brought Brice peace, but not tonight. Not the night before either.

He stirred the campfire until the flames crackled and the fingers of fire reached higher into the sky. Every time something had gone wrong in his life, he'd been able to escape into nature. Live alone for a couple days while his head cleared. The habit dated back to when he was nine years old and his father had come after him with the buckle side of a belt. Brice traced the scar on his cheek. He'd figured living in the wild was better than ever staying under his father's roof again. But after a few days of getting rained on, and once he picked clean a berry bush and hunger attacked him, he'd slunk back home. Thankfully his father had already left for a gambling trip when he returned, but he'd been forced to endure comments from his mother for a week.

Older now, Brice had brought provisions, so hunger pains wouldn't be a problem for a few more days. Besides, it wasn't the same as when he was a child because he wasn't running away anymore. Just clearing his head. That was all. Wasn't it? Brice ran his hand over his face as if he could brush away his tension. A grown man didn't run and hide from his problems. Right?

Bats circled around a nearby pine tree. Night was coming. He would bunk down for one more day. That was all he needed. One more day to get Kendall off his head. To remind himself that his life had progressed just fine before she was a part of it. Although it would take longer to clear her from his heart.

He tucked his hands behind his head and lay back against the hard earth. Tents and sleeping bags weren't his style. Through the pine tree canopy that lined the ravines near the dunes between his property and the land that made up the abandoned summer camp, Brice stared toward the last rays of light. Sunset. *Their time.*

His gut clenched.

One more day alone wouldn't solve his problem. It never did, not really. The escapes bought him time or gave him opportunities to distance himself from people. Building walls to protect himself. He'd always considered that a good thing, but was it?

Brice worked his jaw back and forth. He let out a loud huff.

He and Kendall could never work. Not long term. *Why not?* He had to recite the same reasons he'd been repeating the past two days. Maybe if he said them enough, he'd convince himself. Not likely. But worth another try.

Neither of them came from God-fearing families. That mattered, didn't it? Brice pinched the bridge of his nose. If he had no example to follow, it would be beneficial if the woman he ended up with had been raised in a loving home and had a model she could copy.

A thought niggled at the back of his mind. Wasn't that the role of the church body—to mentor and shepherd each other? He could start a small group based out of the church and invite men like Caleb Beck, Kellen Ashby and Joel Palermo to join him. Guys his age in committed relationships who could learn together what it looked like to be husbands and leaders in their homes. An example didn't have to come from a blood relation. He had plenty of Christian friends who would come alongside him and offer advice and support if he ever did marry.

Brice groaned. He was *supposed* to be convincing himself that breaking things off with Kendall was the right course of action. He shook his head.

She liked to be around people—came alive around large groups—and he would rather spend every weekend either on the lake or back at his cabin tucked away from the crowds. Sure, that hadn't been a problem for them yet, but it would. At some point she'd decide he was a stick-in-the-mud or he'd get sick of going to town festivals. He never wanted to be responsible for holding her back. Not when he'd been accused of doing that in his mother's life.

Besides, Kendall had warned him from their first interaction that she was a serial dater. Told him she always left the guy she was dating. Why would he be any different? Sooner or later, she'd find a reason to cast him aside. She'd see they weren't a good fit or find some reason to leave him. Might as well cut things off before they got to that point.

Then again, they were already past that point, weren't they? They were already to love. At some point between the walks on the beach and watching the sunset side by side, Brice had lost his heart to a woman who had placed herself in the care of the man he disliked the most. That alone meant he couldn't be with her. No matter how much he cared about her.

Brice squeezed his eyes shut. *Sleep.* He just needed sleep. Everything would sort itself out. He would listen to the crickets and frogs and he'd go to sleep and then go back to the life he'd had before he ever met Kendall. Run his shipping business, read his books and spend time with his siblings as if she didn't even live in Goose Harbor.

But the thought of returning to life before Kendall brought him no comfort.

Chapter Fifteen

The bells tinkled as Laura Daniels ducked into Kendall's office. The young woman tucked her hair behind her ears. "Are you and my brother fighting?"

Kendall allowed herself a minute to figure out how she should answer. Technically she and Brice weren't fighting—they had fought once, three days ago. Perhaps it was best to redirect the conversation away from the argument. "What makes you say that?"

"None of us can get in touch with him." Laura shrugged. "He never answers his phone, so whatever, but all the other times he at least leaves a message letting us know what's going on."

He hadn't even spoken to his beloved little sister? That alarmed Kendall, but she didn't want to worry Laura. Kendall tucked her pen into the top desk drawer. "I asked Evan about it earlier. He said taking off isn't abnormal for Brice."

"This time feels different." Laura folded her arms over her chest. "You know, if you guys are fighting, you should go after him."

"Oh, I should, should I?" Kendall locked her desk

and shut down her computer. She'd been at the office for only two hours, but work wasn't going to happen today. "What if your brother doesn't want to be found?"

Laura's brow furrowed. "Everyone wants to be found."

"Maybe so, but how he and I left things... I don't believe it's me he wants finding him."

Laura shook her head. "You know, I thought you were different." Her eyes narrowed, but it looked as if she was holding in tears more than anger. "I thought you'd be good for him and not just another person who would end up hurting him."

Laura was too young; she didn't understand. Kendall sighed. "Believe me, hurting him is the last thing I ever want to do."

"After everything he's been through, Brice needs someone who's willing to fight for him."

That made Kendall pause.

Someone who's willing to fight for him.

For so many years, that had been her desire. She'd never turned it around, though. Never let a man know he was worth sticking through the bad for. She'd spent years waiting for someone to be her champion, but what if it was her turn to be the white knight in someone's life? A message from a church service so many weeks ago flooded back into her mind. She was called to love people. She wasn't called to turn inward at the first sign of possible heartache. And she loved Brice. So she'd fight for him.

Kendall got to her feet. "You're right, Laura. I can't believe I didn't see that before."

Evan offered to go with her to locate Brice, but

she felt that, after everything, this was something she needed to do on her own. After Laura, Evan and Kendall piled into Evan's car, Kendall dialed her father's number and let him know they were heading to Evan's house. Her father had rented a room in town for the next week so they could spend time together.

"For all we know, he may be back at his cabin. We're going to stop there first to see. Laura checked this morning and his cabin was still locked up. But he might have gotten back in the last few hours."

"And if he's not back?" her father asked.

"Then I'm going to go find him. Evan knows his favorite camping spots. He offered to draw a map."

"Please be safe, honey."

"I'll have my cell phone on at all times. I'll be fine."

She gave him both Brice's and Evan's addresses. Laura and Evan invited him to wait with them at Evan's house while Kendall went out searching. If she hadn't returned by nightfall, or if she got lost, she was under strict instructions to stay wherever she was and Evan would come find her. Evan might have been the town flirt, but it turned out he was just as skilled an outdoorsman as his older brother.

With a backpack full of water bottles, granola bars and a few first-aid supplies, Kendall set out a little after noon. Brice and Evan both owned acres and acres of land, and their land backed up to the property that used to serve as a sleepaway summer camp, which was now shut down. Evan had explained that Brice often crossed onto the old camp's property because it was remote and had some of the best fishing for miles. The camp property spanned over six hundred acres of forestland.

Kendall gulped down one of her water bottles and

checked Evan's map. She'd stopped at the first two possible spots and hadn't found any sign of Brice. There were two more spots to check, but both looked far away, deep into the camp property.

It was closing on four in the afternoon when Kendall reached a large ravine. Using branches for handholds, she started to make her way down the steep incline. She'd have to get to the bottom, cross a small stream and then head back up the other side. There didn't look like any other option. Her calves and thigh muscles shook and her lungs ached. Forget workout videos—after this experience, she'd take up hiking to stay in shape.

A low growl of thunder made her stop halfway down. She craned her neck, trying to get a sense for how near the storm was. When she left Evan's home there hadn't been a cloud in sight, but gray blanketed the sky now.

She took her backpack off, set it on the ground and fished out her cell phone. The signal was low, but she pulled up her weather app to check on the storm. A large mass of swirling clouds showed a fast progression over Lake Michigan, and Goose Harbor was directly in its path. Lightning flashed nearby, so bright and close, Kendall jumped. Simultaneously the cell phone slipped from her hand and she lost her footing.

Kendall screamed. She crashed forward, down the steep incline, rocks and branches smashing against her hands, her knees, her back, her ankles. Reaching out desperately, she tried to grab on to something to slow her progression. Her right leg crunched loudly as it caught and twisted in a copse of trees. Her bag tumbled down the hill after her and landed with a loud slosh into the stream.

As she lay caught in the last grouping of trees before the stream, her breath came fast. Pain rippled through her body. Her arms and legs were scraped up, but what concerned her most was the odd angle of her foot. Broken? Shock kept the worst of the discomfort away, but there was one way to know for certain.

Locking a breath in her lungs, Kendall braced her hands on a fallen log and tried to lift herself to standing. When she placed weight on her right foot, it felt as if a hundred burning knives had been shoved into the tendons of her ankle. She cried out and collapsed onto the fallen log.

Her cell phone was long gone, lost somewhere under the brush in the ravine or under the water in the stream. She couldn't call Evan for help and she couldn't walk back to safety with a broken ankle.

A drop of rain hit the side of her face. One drop and then another. The light rain gave way to a downpour. Dark clouds covered any trace of daylight. Thunder rolled, making her jump. *Stay calm.* Someone would come for her; she had to believe that.

Kendall shivered. It would be easy to break down and cry, to give up and feel abandoned. Rain drenched her hair. She crossed her arms, trying to stay warm. Think positive. Focus on the good.

"You've never abandoned me, have You, God? Just like my father… You've loved me and sought after me my whole life." Tears slipped onto her cheeks, mingling with the rainfall. "Even now, You're here with me. Aren't You? Forgive me for ignoring You. For pushing You away. I've been so blind. I can't believe how long I felt alone when You were always there. I'm so sorry for being so stubborn."

The verse that Claire had jotted down for her when Kendall first opened Love on a Dime rushed back... God was doing a new thing. *I am making a way in the wilderness and streams in the desert.* If she surrendered her fear and learned to trust Him fully—even if every human friendship failed her—she'd never have to feel abandoned again.

"I surrender." Kendall tipped her head back, letting the rain wash down her face. "I'm Yours. Forever. I won't forget that again."

"I should have left yesterday," Brice grumbled.

Rain pelted the side of his face as he shoved the rest of his camping gear into his pack. The larger items would slow him down on the walk home, and with the way the storm had rolled in, he'd be wet to the bone by the time he got to his cabin. To speed his journey, he decided to stow the heavier items—a cast-iron skillet and extra cans of food, among other things—beside a tree trunk. He tucked a small tarp over the items and then secured the flap to his bag, slinging it over his shoulder.

Camping and solitude hadn't soothed his soul this time around. His heart and mind felt restless, and he wasn't even certain the unease had to do with Kendall. Sure, their argument had sparked his thoughts, but he had more to sort through than just what to do about what he'd dubbed the *Sesser Situation*. As he searched his heart and mind, he'd found bundle after bundle of hurt feelings tied around barbed wire. Land mines of pain waiting to destroy his world if he dealt with them. Which was why he'd stored the bad memories away, pretending they didn't exist or bother him.

A part of him wondered if he should leave Goose Harbor altogether. Perhaps he should have done that straight after college instead of returning to his hometown. Brice's soul ached for a clean start. He wanted the land mines gone. Goose Harbor held all the reminders of his bad memories. He'd been foolish to ever believe he could make a life here. Who was he to stand against a man like Sesser Atwood?

It wouldn't be difficult to sell his house. If it didn't sell, he could put it up on a rental website for tourists to use while they vacationed. His shipping company wouldn't be hard to divide and sell off in chunks either. The handful of men who worked for him could be placed with the other shipping companies too. Brice had no doubt he could negotiate jobs for all of them.

He stopped walking. Even just considering leaving Goose Harbor made his gut twist into knots. This was his home. This was where he belonged. He'd tried to move away when he attended college, but he hadn't fit anywhere else.

Brice lifted branches out of the way and continued down his well-worn path.

No, he would stay. He couldn't run away every time something bad happened to him. Despite the abuse in his past, he had chosen to stick it out in Goose Harbor even with his father living nearby. If he could share a town with his father and survive, he could deal with passing Kendall on the street every now and then. Couldn't he?

But ignoring the land mines in his heart wouldn't

make them go away. He jammed the heel of his palm into his chest. They'd go off at some point, derailing his life again. If only…if only he could deactivate them. Deal with them and be done with the pain forever.

Forgive.

Kendall had mentioned the word to him so many times the thought came automatically. The barbed wire in his heart and thoughts, the baggage taking up all the room inside—he was so busy hanging on to all the bad things, he had no room for the good God brought into his life.

His hurt might be legitimate, but allowing it to hinder his life wasn't. In the past, he thought he had moved on. Buried everything. But in truth, he'd never forgiven the people in his past; therefore, as Kendall had suggested, the bad feelings had taken hold of his heart.

There were so many people he needed to forgive. Not because they deserved it—no one on earth deserved forgiveness, including him—but because his soul couldn't heal until he forgave them. His dad for a lifetime of abuse. His mom for making him feel he should never have been born. Andrew, his brother, for bailing on their family without a word. Audra for the scar of rejection. Sesser for all the pain he'd wrought on the Daniels family.

And himself… Brice needed to forgive himself. For not being able to fix his family. For not being able to save those he loved from hurt. For years of bitterness he hid behind being introverted.

Ignoring the rain and the mud, Brice dropped to

his knees and wove his fingers into the long grasses. "Forgive me," he whispered. Rain beat against his back and streamed down his nose. "Please, forgive me."

Chapter Sixteen

Kendall's skin was numb to the pinpricking light rain that found its way to her through holes in the canopy. Storms always came like that. First with a rush of power and destruction and then they ended with a shower of blessing. Clouds still imprisoned the sun, but that mattered little; it would set any minute. Soon it would be dark and cold and she'd have to wait until morning to be found.

But she wasn't alone. God was with her. Even now.

Lord... I know You're here with me. I don't doubt that. You'll be here with me all night. But...but please send help. If Evan or anyone is out looking for me, please guide their steps. The ground is so slick still. Keep them safe.

Wind swept down the ravine and Kendall shivered. The tank top and shorts that had seemed so sensible for hiking during the day offered little protection against the coming night. About an hour ago, the intense pain in her ankle had gone away, wearing down into a constant pulse of discomfort. She'd tried to stand again, but that had sent another wash of agony through her leg. Sitting and waiting was best.

"Kendall!" A voice came from above. It was followed by the sound of someone slopping through mud. Brice was at her side quicker than she would have thought anyone could descend the wet hillside safely. He dropped to his knees in front of where she sat on the log. His gaze raked over her face; his lips were parted. "Why? I don't understand."

"How did you find me?"

"I was up there. Praying." He pointed up the hill. "When I stood up, I happened to glance down here. I spotted you right away. What are you doing out here?"

Brice. Strong and steady Brice. He was here and either he was so shocked to find her in the middle of the forest that he'd forgotten to be upset with her, or he was no longer angry. *Please let it be the second option.*

She hesitated for a heartbeat before laying her hands on his shoulders. *Just say it. Speak honestly. Be vulnerable.* "I came after you."

He splayed his hands against the tree bark on either side of her and tilted his head to meet her eyes. "Why, though? Is everything okay? Is someone—"

"Everything's not okay." She leaned toward him. "Not when you and I are at odds."

He nodded, once. "I was such a mule, Kendall. So, so stupid. If you'll take me back, I'd like to make it up to you and find a way for us to be together. Would it…? Is it possible you could forgive me?" His head dropped and he rested his forehead against her knee. "I understand if you don't want to."

She worked her fingers into his hair. "I forgive you.

And, Brice?" She tipped his head back so she could see his gorgeous green eyes. "I love you."

A sharp intake of breath parted his lips. He reached toward her and gently brushed a wet tangle of hair from her face. Then he rested his palm against her cheek. "I love you too."

For a minute they sat there, grinning at each other in the twilight.

"Let's head home," Brice said, rising to his feet and offering his hand.

Kendall shook her head. "I can't." She held up her ankle. "I think it might be broken."

He gaped at her leg and dropped back down beside her. "Oh, Kendall. You should have told me about that first." Gripping her calf, he lifted her foot to rest on his thigh and gingerly touched her ankle. "Does this hurt?"

Fire erupted under her skin. She hissed. "A lot."

He peeled off his backpack and dropped it next to the log. "I'm going to carry you out."

Placing a hand on his chest, she made him pause. "Think this through. It's a long way back. It would be easier with a couple more people and a stretcher. Leave me here and—"

"Leaving you is out of the question."

"Brice."

"I can do this," he urged. "Let me take care of you."

"Okay." She nodded and then pointed at his backpack. "If you leave your gear behind, it might get ruined."

"You're more important." Hands under her knees and behind her shoulders, he scooped her up and settled her against his chest. "Loop your arm around my neck."

"Gladly." She sighed and leaned her head on his shoulder. *Thank You*, she prayed. *Thank You for taking care of me. Thank You for all You're doing in my life. Thank You for being a God who creates streams in the desert.*

Brice's arms burned from carrying Kendall, but his cabin wasn't far now.

She lifted her head from his shoulder. "If you want to set me down for a while, we could rest and start back again later."

Didn't Kendall realize by now? As long as it was within his power, he was never letting go of her again.

He tightened his hold on her. "We're close."

"I met my father." Her breath warmed his jawline. "He saw an article about my business in a newspaper and showed up on my doorstep."

Brice clenched his teeth, working through what to say. Like her mother, was her father after money too? If anyone came up against Kendall, they'd have to get through Brice first. He'd be her protector from now on, as long as she wanted him to be. "Are you considering this a good thing?"

"My mom kidnapped me, Brice. Kidnapped!" She launched into the background. Her mother moving them all the time and how her dad had always been looking for her. "He loves me. He never stopped looking for me. Brice." Her arm resting across his shoulders tensed as she got excited. "I was never abandoned. That was my perception, but it wasn't the truth."

"I'm so glad you get to have a relationship with him now."

She went on, telling him about her three siblings. Her dad had invited her out to Ohio to meet everyone, and Kendall was planning to go within the month. "But more than all that, I came to the same realization about God."

"And what realization is that?"

"He never abandoned me either. I blamed Him for so much. I kept holding on to this idea that I was all alone in the world and had to take care of myself because no one else would if I didn't, but that's so wrong. I was completely wrong." She shook her head in a sad way. "God's always been there. He's been taking care of me all along and I haven't been giving Him credit for it."

"That's amazing, and you're right—neither of us has ever walked alone. That's powerful." Brice's cabin came into view. Lights burned through the window, letting him know that either Evan or Laura had decided to check on his place while he'd been gone. "While we're on the subject, I took your advice."

"Oh?" She smoothed a hand down the back of his head. "And what advice was that?"

"I forgave everyone." His gaze captured hers. "You were right. Without realizing it, I'd been holding on to so many grudges. They were clogging up my heart— there wasn't room for the love I wanted to have in there. There is now, though." He stopped walking so he could focus solely on her. "I love you so much. I hope you realize that."

She answered him with a smile and then leaned in, pressing her lips to his.

His front door banged against its hinges. "They're here! They're back," Laura yelled. "And they're kissing!"

Kendall tossed back her head and laughed.

"Take it easy," he teased. "We need to get you to the hospital."

Kendall's laughter faded. "I need to clean up first. Please don't make me go looking like a drowned rat."

He was in the middle of telling her how beautiful he thought she was when Evan and another man rushed out of the house, ushering them both inside as they asked a hundred questions. Brice helped Kendall to the bathroom and then left her in the care of his sister. Before the door closed Kendall whispered she loved him. Brice went downstairs, his heart soaring with a newfound lightness now that it finally had room for all the love God had surrounded him with when he wasn't even looking.

Thankfully Laura had spare sets of clothing at Brice's house and offered Kendall her choice from the drawer. The shirt was a little snug, but the sweatpants were a good fit. Once she was dressed, Brice rushed upstairs, carried her back down and set her on the wide couch near the fireplace. Laura brought over an ice pack and her father urged them to head to the hospital.

Brice placed a pillow on top of the coffee table so she could elevate her ankle. "If you're hungry, Evan made some noodle something while you were showering. If not, we need to get you to a doctor." He rested his arm on the back of the couch as his gaze assessed her. It took everything in her not to lean into his chest again and kiss him. But there were other people nearby, so she held back. There would be time for affection later.

Evan had explained that when he hadn't been able to reach her phone, he and Laura had moved to Brice's cabin to wait, knowing that would be the place they'd probably return to. The storm hit too fast for Evan to have realized it was coming, although he apologized profusely for sending her out into the wilderness without checking the radar first. Worried when the rain started, her father had called Evan and then decided to join them at Brice's cabin to wait for her. Evan and her father were setting out to go search when she and Brice had returned.

Kendall jutted her chin toward the kitchen, where the three others were huddled around the island eating. "I'll eat before we go. Who knows how long we'll be at the ER? And I haven't had anything since my morning coffee." She patted her stomach.

Evan scooped food onto a plate and carried it over. Steam curled from the top of perfectly browned cheese layered over stuffed shells. "And it's not noodle something, as my bear of a brother so eloquently put it. These, my dear woman, are chicken pesto shells. Eat and be amazed." He bowed as he handed her the plate.

Kendall shook her head. The man would always be a charmer, but he couldn't hold a candle to his older brother, not in Kendall's eyes.

Brice rolled his eyes, watching his brother walk back to the kitchen. "If you can get past his smugness, he's actually a really good guy."

Kendall took a bite of the pasta shells. The tangy flavor of pesto rushed over her taste buds. "And a great cook! I could eat ten of these."

"I'll have him pack some for the hospital." Brice laughed.

"Let's not go that far." Kendall bumped her shoulder into his. "Evan might get an even bigger head if we rave too much." She polished off the four shells within minutes.

Brice held out a hand to take her plate. "Should we head out?"

"Look," she whispered and pointed toward the kitchen, where Laura, Evan and her father were laughing together. "For my entire life I felt cheated because I didn't have a family. It was only me and Mom, and more often than not, she was MIA. But we have family, Brice. Those people in there, they care about us."

He nodded. "They love us. All three of them want what's best for us."

"The best for me is you." She laced her fingers through his and pressed a kiss to the back of his hand.

"About Sesser..." Brice cleared his throat.

Her fingers tensed. "I can't break my partnership with him."

"I know. It was wrong of me to ask that."

"I trust you—you know that, right? If you say Sesser is bad news, I believe you. I'll be careful. I won't get in deeper with him than I already am, but I can't quit my business."

"I agree. And I want to keep doing sunset cruises."

"But what about the tourist tax? You'll never be able to save enough to pursue your dream. To build your own pier."

"I will." His hand covered hers. "I'm going to beat him, but I'm going to do it honorably. I'll pay his taxes and fees. It'll take longer, but I'm still determined to thrive in this town. Sesser doesn't get to steal that from me. Not where my business is concerned, but even more so, not when it comes to you."

Kendall nodded, pressing her lips together as she held in happy tears. She was overwhelmed by Brice's love.

He rubbed his thumb over the back of her hand. "Let's get you to the hospital now. We need to make you well."

She laughed as he scooped her up in his arms again. Laura ran to get the door for them.

"Brice." She caught his wrist and tugged him close when he set her in the passenger seat of his vehicle. "I've never been better in my life. I'm so blessed. I feel so overwhelmed by it all."

"We've both been blessed. You're the greatest blessing in my life." Brice dropped a kiss on her lips before closing the door. He called something to Evan, who was on the porch, and then climbed into the car, backing them out of the driveway.

Everything in life wasn't perfect. Her mother and she were still at odds and might always be. Her credit was still a disaster from what her mother had done. She was in debt to Sesser Atwood, a businessman she now realized she'd need to be wary of. Brice's parents were both still abusive in their own way. She couldn't make that better for Brice. And his business would continue to struggle. The other brother of the Daniels family—Andrew—was still missing.

Life would never be perfect. There would always be struggles and pain.

But in the midst of everything, there would be blessings. Streams in the desert.

Epilogue

Kendall couldn't keep the smile off her face when she turned off the highway for the exit that led to Goose Harbor.

Home.

She'd never grow tired of that concept. After a life spent wandering, she finally had a home. But the smile was more for Brice than the fact that she was almost back in Goose Harbor after two weeks of being away. She couldn't wait to see him.

Kendall had waited a month to make the trip out to meet her siblings and her stepmother. Waiting for the doctor's clearance to drive had been torture. Brice had offered to drive her to Ohio, but she had needed him to stay back to take care of their Friday night sunset cruises.

Meeting her siblings, being welcomed into a family and getting to know her father had been amazing. But the trip hadn't been all smiles. At her father's urging, he and she had taken a few days to drive to Kentucky so Kendall could finally file a police report against her mother for identity theft. It was the only way to clear Kendall's financial history, and she needed that in order to break her partnership with Sesser Atwood. She'd need to show her solid financial history, which required the proof of filing a report with the police, in order to secure a new loan—one to pay back Sesser and be done with him for good.

As much as Kendall hated the thought of her mother being arrested, Mom had made her choices and whatever consequences came weren't Kendall's fault. She had to keep telling herself that. Besides, since her dad had appeared in Goose Harbor, Kendall's mom had taken off. No one had heard from her since. Perhaps the police wouldn't find her.

Kendall drove slowly through the downtown area and parked near the café. She'd made it back in time for this week's Friday night sunset cruise. Locking her car, Kendall turned and headed down the pier, her heart skipping as she rounded to where Brice's paddle wheeler was docked.

Brice stood in the doorway, wearing a full tuxedo. His face broke into a goofy big smile when he saw her. "Come here." He opened his arms. "I've missed you."

Kendall launched toward him, wrapping her arms around his waist as she laughed. "What's with the tux? Hey." She stepped back and surveyed the boat. "Where are all the people?"

If it was possible, Brice's smile widened. "Just us tonight."

He led her on board and started the engine.

"Brice?"

"Relax, Kendall. Enjoy the ride." He steered the boat into deep waters.

For a few minutes Kendall hung out near the railing, watching the setting sun and the calm water, but then she circled back to where Brice was, came up behind him and wrapped her arms around his middle. Her hand found his heartbeat. Strong and steady, the exact words she'd use to describe this man. She'd missed him so much.

Brice cut the engine and turned in her arms. "I had this whole night planned." He suddenly looked nervous. "And now I can't wait... Kendall?"

"Are you—" Kendall's mouth dropped open. "Are you doing what I think you're doing? You're in a tux. You're asking me to... Brice, I look like a vagabond!" She still wore the jeans and shirt she'd been driving in all day.

"You are, easily, the most beautiful woman I've ever met. Inside and out." He ran his hand over her hair. "The last two weeks made me realize that I never want to be apart from you again. I wanted to watch the sunset with you today—"

"Because sunsets belong to us." She rested her hands on his chest, looking up into the face she loved.

"But that's just it. I don't want only your sunsets. I want your days. Your nights. Your early mornings. I want every part of the days to be ours. Marry me, Kendall? Say you'll marry me," he whispered the end. "I love you. I will love you every moment for the rest of our lives."

"Yes." Kendall fisted her hands into his suit coat and leaned back and yelled, "Yes!" Unable to contain her joy, she laughed.

Brice fished a ring out of his pocket. "I was supposed to get on one knee. I was supposed to—"

She snatched the ring and slipped it onto her finger.

Then she kissed him soundly. "It was perfect. Every second of your proposal was perfect." She kissed him again, for good measure. "I love you. So much."

Brice extended his hand. "Watch the sunset with me?"

Kendall laced her fingers through his. "Every single one."

* * * * *

Pick up these other GOOSE HARBOR *stories
from Jessica Keller:
Love is in big supply on the shores
of Lake Michigan*

*THE WIDOWER'S SECOND CHANCE
THE FIREMAN'S SECRET
THE SINGLE DAD NEXT DOOR*

Available now from Love Inspired!

Find more great reads at www.LoveInspired.com

Dear Reader,

Loving people is hard work. When you choose love, you open yourself up to being hurt. And the truth is, anytime you love you will get hurt. Every time. That's because no human or human relationship is perfect, so despite trying to protect ourselves, we will end up hurting each other at one point or another.

Choosing to love, knowing that you'll get hurt... can be scary. It can even seem downright pointless. Wouldn't it be better to keep people at an arm's distance? Be friendly enough, but just not open? That would be easier. Logical. Safer.

But Jesus leans in and whispers, "Love anyway." See, we are called to love. It's a command. Christ tells us to love one another because He knows a life that isn't spent loving others will leave us feeling unfulfilled. Love is the courageous choice every time. This world will break our hearts, but that is where grace and mercy come in and fill the cracks that hurt creates.

Thank you for spending time with Kendall and Brice. I'm so happy they were able to move beyond the baggage from their pasts and both choose to walk in love going forward. Make sure to come back to Goose Harbor often and discover what's happening in the lives of familiar faces as well as meet new friends.

I love interacting with readers. Connect with me on my Facebook Author Page, on Twitter and at www.JessicaKellerBooks.com.

Dream Big!
Jess

COMING NEXT MONTH FROM
Love Inspired®

Available August 23, 2016

HIS AMISH SWEETHEART
Amish Hearts • by Jo Ann Brown

When Esther Stoltzfus's childhood crush, Nathaniel Zook, returns to their Amish community and asks for help with his farm—and an orphaned boy in need—will their friendship blossom into a happily-ever-after?

THE RANCHER'S HOMECOMING
The Prodigal Ranch • by Arlene James

Rex Billings has come home to Straight Arrow Ranch to help his ailing father, and is in desperate need of a housekeeper. With her fine cooking, single mom Callie Deviner seems the perfect candidate—for the job and to be his partner for life.

REUNITING WITH THE COWBOY
Texas Cowboys • by Shannon Taylor Vannatter

Having rodeo cowboy Cody Warren move in next door might just be Ally Curtis's second chance with the boy who got away. But can she trust that the charming bull rider is ready to settle down for good?

FALLING FOR THE SINGLE DAD
by Lisa Carter

Single dad Weston Clark is taken aback when his daughter forms an instant bond with veterinarian Caroline Duer. As they work together to save a wounded sea turtle, can the former coast guard commander make room in his life for a new wife?

THE SOLDIER'S SURPRISE FAMILY
by Jolene Navarro

Former soldier Garrett Kincaid had no plans for a family, until he discovers he has a son he never knew existed. Now his child and the lovely new nanny he's hired are quickly capturing his heart.

HER TEXAS HERO
Texas Sweetheart • by Kat Brookes

Single mom Audra Marshall realizes that her fresh start means accepting Carter Cooper's help in fixing up her new house—so she trades home-cooked meals for labor. But can she exchange the hurts from her past for a new chance at forever?

LOOK FOR THESE AND OTHER LOVE INSPIRED BOOKS WHEREVER BOOKS ARE SOLD, INCLUDING MOST BOOKSTORES, SUPERMARKETS, DISCOUNT STORES AND DRUGSTORES.

LICNM0816

REQUEST YOUR FREE BOOKS!

2 FREE INSPIRATIONAL NOVELS

PLUS 2
FREE
MYSTERY GIFTS

Love Inspired®

YES! Please send me 2 FREE Love Inspired® novels and my 2 FREE mystery gifts (gifts are worth about $10). After receiving them, if I don't wish to receive any more books, I can return the shipping statement marked "cancel." If I don't cancel, I will receive 6 brand-new novels every month and be billed just $4.99 per book in the U.S. or $5.49 per book in Canada. That's a saving of at least 17% off the cover price. It's quite a bargain! Shipping and handling is just 50¢ per book in the U.S. and 75¢ per book in Canada.* I understand that accepting the 2 free books and gifts places me under no obligation to buy anything. I can always return a shipment and cancel at any time. Even if I never buy another book, the two free books and gifts are mine to keep forever.

105/305 IDN GH5P

Name	(PLEASE PRINT)

Address	Apt. #

City	State/Prov.	Zip/Postal Code

Signature (if under 18, a parent or guardian must sign)

Mail to the **Reader Service:**
IN U.S.A.: P.O. Box 1867, Buffalo, NY 14240-1867
IN CANADA: P.O. Box 609, Fort Erie, Ontario L2A 5X3

**Are you a subscriber to Love Inspired® books
and want to receive the larger-print edition?
Call 1-800-873-8635 or visit www.ReaderService.com.**

* Terms and prices subject to change without notice. Prices do not include applicable taxes. Sales tax applicable in N.Y. Canadian residents will be charged applicable taxes. Offer not valid in Quebec. This offer is limited to one order per household. Not valid for current subscribers to Love Inspired books. All orders subject to credit approval. Credit or debit balances in a customer's account(s) may be offset by any other outstanding balance owed by or to the customer. Please allow 4 to 6 weeks for delivery. Offer available while quantities last.

Your Privacy—The Reader Service is committed to protecting your privacy. Our Privacy Policy is available online at www.ReaderService.com or upon request from the Reader Service.

We make a portion of our mailing list available to reputable third parties that offer products we believe may interest you. If you prefer that we not exchange your name with third parties, or if you wish to clarify or modify your communication preferences, please visit us at www.ReaderService.com/consumerschoice or write to us at Reader Service Preference Service, P.O. Box 9062, Buffalo, NY 14240-9062. Include your complete name and address.

LI15

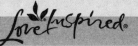
"Are you sure you want Jacob to stay with you?" Esther asked.

"I'm sure staying at my farm is best for him now," Nathaniel said. "The boy needs something to do to get his mind off the situation, and the alpacas can help."

Nathaniel held his hand out to assist Esther onto the seat of the buggy.

She regarded him with surprise, and he had to fight not to smile. Her reaction reminded him of Esther the Pester from their childhood, who'd always asserted she could do anything the older boys did…and all by herself.

Despite that, she accepted his help. The scent of her shampoo lingered in his senses. He was tempted to hold on to her soft fingers, but he released them as soon as she was sitting. He was too aware of the *kinder* and other women gathered behind her.

She picked up the reins and leaned toward him. "If it becomes too difficult for you, bring him to our house."

"We'll be fine." At that moment, he meant it. When her bright blue eyes were close to his, he couldn't imagine being anything but fine.

Then she looked away, and the moment was over. She slapped the reins and drove the wagon toward the road. He watched it go. A sudden shiver ran along him. The breeze was damp and chilly, something he hadn't noticed while gazing into Esther's pretty eyes.

The sound of the rattling wagon vanished in the distance, and he turned to see Jacob standing by the fence, his fingers through the chicken wire again in the hope an alpaca would come to him. The *kind* had no idea of what could lie ahead for him.

Take him into Your hands, Lord. He's going to need Your comfort in the days to come. Make him strong to face what the future brings, but let him be weak enough to accept help from us.

Taking a deep breath, Nathaniel walked toward the boy. He'd agreed to take care of Jacob and offer him a haven at the farm. Now he had to prove he could.

Don't miss
HIS AMISH SWEETHEART by Jo Ann Brown,
available September 2016 wherever
Love Inspired® books and ebooks are sold.

www.LoveInspired.com

LIEXP0816

A young woman desperately needs a husband to avoid a life of drudgery. Will the handsome stranger in town be her Prince Charming?

Read on for a sneak preview of
TEXAS CINDERELLA,
the next book in Winnie Griggs's miniseries
TEXAS GROOMS.

"Are you talking to the horses?"

Cassie Lynn turned her head to see a freckle-faced boy of six eyeing her curiously.

"Of course. They're friends of mine." Then she smiled. "I don't think we've met before?"

The boy shook his head. "We just got to town a little while ago. I'm Noah."

"Glad to meet you, Noah. I'm Cassie Lynn."

"My uncle Riley likes to talk to horses, too."

"Sounds like a smart man." She held out her apple slices and nodded toward the two mares. "Would you like to feed them?"

The boy smiled and took the slices. He stepped up on the fence so he could lean over the top rail.

She smiled as the boy stroked the mare's muzzle. "I see you've done this before."

The boy nodded. "Uncle Riley has a real fine horse."

Well, at least she knew the boy wasn't alone. "Are you visiting someone here or do you and your folks plan to settle down in Turnabout?"

The boy shook his head. "We don't know anyone here.

And I don't have folks anymore. It's just me, Pru and Uncle Riley."

Before she could form a response, they were interrupted.

"Noah, what are you doing out here?"

Noah quickly turned and lost his footing. Cassie Lynn moved to stop his fall and ended up landing in the dirt on her backside with Noah on her lap.

"Are you all right?"

She looked up to see a man she didn't know helping Noah stand up. But the concerned frown on his face was focused on her.

"I'm a bit dusty, but otherwise fine," she said with a rueful smile.

He stooped down, studying her as if he didn't quite believe her.

She met his gaze and found herself looking into the deepest, greenest eyes she'd ever seen.

Cassie Lynn found herself entranced by the genuine concern and intelligence reflected in the newcomer's expression. It made her temporarily forget that she was sitting in the dirty livery yard.

"Can I help you up?"

She quickly nodded. "Yes, thank you." Hoping there was no visible sign of the warmth she felt in her cheeks, Cassie Lynn held out her hand.

He took it in his, and she had the strangest feeling that she could hold on to that hand forever.

Don't miss
TEXAS CINDERELLA by Winnie Griggs,
available September 2016 wherever
Love Inspired® Historical books and ebooks are sold.

www.LoveInspired.com